WONDER TALES
FROM
BALTIC WIZARDS

To

ALBERT von JULIN

A Patriot of Finland

FOREWORD

WIZARDS IN FOLK-LORE

ENCHANTMENTS, Wizards, Witches, Magic Spells, Nixy Queens, Giants, Fairy White Reindeer, and glittering Treasures flourish in these tales from the Baltic Lands—Lapland (both Finnish and Scandinavian), Finland, Estonia, Latvia, and Lithuania.

And their setting is the Long Winter Night with its brilliant play of Northern Lights over the snow-covered tundra; or the brief Arctic summer—its sun burning night and day—with its birds, flowers, insect-clouds, singing waters, and almost tropic heat; or the golden sunshine of the southern amber coast.

But it is the Northern Lights themselves, flashing and flaming through the dark heavens, that cast their mystic weirdness over many of these tales molded by the peculiar imagination of the Asiatic and European East Baltic folks.

The farther our stories draw south from Lapland, the lower sink the Northern Lights, and the less their influence on folk-tales, till at last they merge with the warmer lights of Lithuania the amber-land. Wizards and wizardry abound in Lappish, Finnish, and Estonian tales, Witches appear more often in Latvian and Lithuanian ones. And in all these countries except Lapland, many European folk-tale themes, which we know in the Grimm collection, are found in new forms.

The Latvians and Lithuanians are Aryan peoples. The Lapps came from Asia, and the Finns and Estonians are descendants of the Finno-

Ugric tribes emigrating from Asia to the Baltic shores. The Lapps and Finns are famous for their Wizards and wizardry. Even today some Lapps use magic incantations which are peculiar admixtures of ancient heathen superstitions and Christian ideas. The modern Lapp who is only half taught in the Gospel of Christ the Lord, which frees from superstition, is a strange compound of heathen survivals accentuated by the hard conditions of life within the Arctic Circle.

And bound by chains of superstition, the Lapp shows little progress. He is gradually being absorbed by neighboring races. It is far different with the Finns. Naturally more progressive, in co-operation with their compatriots, the Swedish-Finlanders, they have produced a modern Republic which in progress and culture is comparable to any European state. United with Finland is a large part of Lapland. Estonia, too, is a progressive modern Republic, as are Latvia and Lithuania.

But to return to Wizards in folk-lore. It is surprising that such an entertaining type of wonder tale as "Aladdin and the Wonderful Lamp," which delights our children's fancy, should have its roots in one of the most repellent of soul-slaveries—Shamanism.

The shaman, wizard, witch-doctor, heathen priest, medicine man—by whatever name he be called—was and still is among some heathen tribes a force controlling with iron grip tribal life, both of chiefs and people. By of his art, the shaman, usually a professional trickster, works on the fear, credulity, and natural religious instinct of his ignorant dupes.

By howlings and whistlings, hideous maskings, capers and leapings, beating of gongs and drums, incantations to bad or good spirits, and by hocus-pocus healing and some real curative knowledge, the shaman manages to keep the helpless folk in trembling terror of his power over their lives. He is an enemy to progress and civilization.

Shamanism in some form is prevalent in all parts of the world, among Asiatics, European Arctic peoples, Africans, American Indians including Eskimos, also Afro-Americans, and the savage islanders of the seas. It is not possible in this short Foreword, to discuss Shamanism in all its phases, with its holdover in mediaeval and modern witchcraft revivals.

But, just as many delightful poetic fairy tales have had their beginnings in pagan myths, so from professional wizardry have descended a variety and host of fascinating tales which, under the magic brush of a light and playful fancy, have taken on the colors of wonder to delight modern children.

The selections in this book come from German and English sources. There is a mass of East Baltic folk-lore and folk-tales in these languages, from which to choose. In the languages of Finland and Estonia alone, may be found more than 33,000 native folk-melodies, 55,000 folk tales, 125,000 riddles, 135,000 superstitions, 215,000 proverbs, 200,000 folk songs. This gives but a feeble idea of the extent of Baltic folk-lore.

The racial groupings of tales here, are interesting to compare—primitive Lapp legends; richly poetic creations of the Finns and their kindred, the Estonians; European types of wonder story, product of the Aryan Letts and Lithuanians. Each group holds its distinctive place in the history of peoples.

And what a variety of selections is here!—prose epitomes of the musical hero tales, and imaginative wonder stories of Finland and Estonia; weird Lapp ideas; romantic legends and wonder tales from Latvia and Lithuania, all so delightful to children. Repulsive tales have been omitted. The wonder tales, with few exceptions, are literally translated. Several rambling ones are shortened. The article, "What Happened to Some Lapp Children," is composed of bits of assembled folklore. The half-title original verses are in Kalevala metre, while the little connecting stories, also original, follow the changing seasons of Lapland, and are woven from bits of folk-wisdom and custom.

All these colorful tales, together with The Tiny History of the Baltic Sea, and The Tiny Dictionary of Strange East Baltic Things will, we hope, charm the children and help them to understand and like the countries and peoples of our East Baltic neighbors.

Mr. Victor G. Candell, our American artist, was born in Hungary and has travelled in the East Baltic. For these pictures he has made a special study of the art motif of these lands, and has rendered them with a wealth of detail. He is an associate of Mr. Willy Pogany.

And this book is dedicated to my friend, Albert von Julin, an iron-master and patriot of Finland, who during the revolution after the late War, was killed, because of his ardent patriotic principles. It was he who first interested me in Finland and the Baltic. So may this book pay honor to his memory.

FRANCES JENKINS OLCOTT

CONTENTS

ESTONIA, WISE AND FREE,
LAND OF WONDER LEGENDS

LATVIA OF FEAST OF FLOWERS, AND,
COURLAND, GOD'S OWN LITTLE COUNTRY

LITHUANIA OF THE FRAGRANT AMBER

INTERESTING THINGS

THE MAGIC DRUM CALLS YOU!

BOOM! BOOM! BOOM! BEAT! BEAT! BEAT!

In Lapland when the Arctic Storm Wind roars down from the mountains and blows through the valleys and over the tundra, comes the call of the Magic Drum.

Do you hear it on the wind? Do you hear its beat! beat! beat! and the grinding of the Wizard's teeth as he beats! beats! beats!

Long, long ago, with chanting and magic and drum-beating came the Great Wizard Nischergurje down from the mountains. Tree-tall, tree-straight was he, clad in the softest skins of the white reindeer. He was girded with the Wizard Belt of Might, and on his feet were soft-soled shoes. From his right wrist hung his gold drum-hammer, and his left hand held the Magic Drum. Beat! Beat! Beat!

Down from the everlasting snow-peaks he came to visit the Lapp people. He saw smoke curling up from their tents in the valley, where reindeer were digging moss out of the snow, with their hoofs.

And the Lapp people—little children, men, and women—ran and thronged about him in welcome. The finest reindeer-skins they spread for his seat in front of their tents, and the choicest reindeer flesh they dipped from their cooking pots to feast the Great Wizard.

And he sang to the people his Magic Words of the days when stones were gold and silver, and he sang:

"I have learned the secret of the foxes. I have the strength of Honey-Paw the bear, of Thick-Pelt-Old-Man-of-the-Forest. Fleeter am I than the snarling wolf. I know the place of hidden treasures. I know the secret of the Forest.

"Now will I send forth my Magic Call to summon my Comrades, the Four Ancient Wizards of the South Baltic Lands!"

And see! As the great Wizard Nischergurgje beat! beat! beat! on his Magic Drum, and tapped! tapped! tapped! on his Magic Drum, the Storm Wind blew fiercer. On its flapping wings came riding the Four Ancient Wizards!

Kauko, Red-Haired Wizard of Finland of the Thousand Lakes and Thousand Isles:

Sarvik with woolly white hair, back like an oak and lolling red tongue— from Estonia's rocky coast:

Kurbads giant-strong, with yellow eyeballs and green hair from Latvia of the crystal streams:

Jakamas with bushy golden head, pointed eyes, and apple-red cheeks— from Lithuania of the fragrant amber.

And each carried his own Magic Drum. Beat! Beat! Beat!

And the Four Ancient Wizards, grinding their teeth, whistling, and howling, seated themselves on the snow before the Chief Wizard of them all, the great Nischergurgje.

And he, the tree-tall, tree-straight one, struck his Drum with a rolling and a roaring, and bade the Four Ancient Wizards be still, so that the Lapp people might listen to his Tales of Wonder.

And the Four Ancient Wizards were still, and the people waited. Listen to Nischergurgje!

BEAT! BEAT! BEAT! BOOM! BOOM! BOOM!

FROM LAPLAND OF AURORA COLORS WHITE SILENCE MOSSY TUNDRAS AND HILLS WHERE REINDEER FEED

Lapland's Children, they are singing,
Chant the Children of the Northland!
While the winter nights grow longer,
And the days have no returnings;
And the Long Nights shimmer whitely
O'er the icy wastes and tundras;
Where the Reindeer nibble mosses,
Silver lichens 'neath the snowfall.

Lapland's Children still are singing,
Chant the Children of the Northland!
"See! across the sky are sweeping
Amber lights that shift and flutter,
Rosy arc and violet flashings,
Flames that dart and veils that tremble,
O'er the sky they move and glimmer!"

Lapland's Children still are singing,
Chant the Children of the Northland!
"See! O see! The Merry Dancers,
Towards the zenith streaming, leaping!

In the heart of the Aurora,
Dance the Merry Baltic Wizards,
From the Lands of Baltic Wonders,
From the Lands of Baltic Magic!"

THE BATTLE OF THE WIZARDS

BOOM! BOOM! BOOM! BEAT! BEAT! BEAT!
Listen to Nischergurgje!

Far, far away in Lapland of the Many Wizards, beyond the Arctic Circle, in mid-winter, it is one Long Night. But what a night!

There is silence. The stars sparkle in the vast, dark sky. A soft white shimmer glows over the fields of ice and snow covering tundra, valley, and hill. Deep ice binds the lakes and streams.

Then see! Upward across the sky sweep wondrous lights. Amber-colored veils shimmer to and fro, rosy draperies, garlands, and streamers red, orange, yellow, green, blue, and violet, dart, dance, sway, shift, wave, and leap across the sky; flare up and die down, then spring up again woven all of rainbow colors.

And the little, dark children of Lapland of the many Wizards and much Magic, are filled with mystery. They listen for the Call of the Magic Drum, and they watch the Aurora Lights, and say:

"See! the warriors are fighting!"

In the long, long ago, the Wizard Nischergurgje, chanting Magic Spells with whistlings and drum-beatings, came wandering over the frozen marshes. Under a crooked pine tree he sat down to rest, and to boil his dinner of reindeer flesh.

And while he was waiting for the cooking pot to simmer, he heard something creak—crack—creak above his head. He looked up. Through the crooked boughs, an evil face grinned at him. It was Schlipme's—the Wicked Wizard of the Wicked Moon Daughter.

Then Nischergurgje quickly muttered a Spell, and the Wicked Wizard tumbled to the ground.

"Wicked Schlipme," said the Great Wizard, "Servant of the Wicked Moon Daughter, of the caved-in forehead, crooked mouth, and pale, cruel lips that splutter curses! See! My Spell has taken from you all your power."

"Nischergurgje," snarled the Wicked Wizard, "my Magic is still strong. I can call on the Moon Spirits to destroy you."

"Your Black Art does not frighten me," answered Nischergurgje.

Then the Wicked Schlipme stood up, and by his Black Art grew and grew, taller and taller, to great stature. In his hand he swung a terrible club made of a spruce tree.

"I will grind you to powder as fine as the snow on the hillside," he roared. "Tremble before me!"

"See what my Good Magic will do!" said Nischergurgje.

And he muttered a Spell, and he, too, grew and grew, taller and taller and yet taller. Greater he was than the Wicked Wizard. The tallest pines in the forest scarce reached his knees. The highest peaks of the mountains scarce touched his waist. His chest and shoulders were hid among the clouds. His chin pushed the moon. His eyes glared into the sun.

"You have taken my strength from me!" cried Schlipme in fear.

Then they changed themselves into dreadful Storm Clouds. They rushed upon each other. They closed in fierce combat. A mighty roaring was heard. The sky was black.

Nischergurgje uttered a terrible Spell, and Schlipme fell in a heap to earth.

"Again you have taken my strength from me!" cried the Wicked Wizard.

Once more the two Wizards changed their forms. They became two great, horned reindeer. They battled over the frozen snow of the hillside.

The whole forest echoed with the loud clashing of their antlers. The trampling of their hoofs shook the earth.

Then the Wicked Wizard was too weak to fight more. He changed himself into a great snake writhing on the ground. Nischer gurgje, too, became a snake. They twined and twisted. Their angry hissing could be heard afar off. Their dripping fangs were dreadful to see.

Then suddenly the Wicked Wizard stretched himself upon the ground as if dead. In the twinkling of an eye he became a mighty bird. He soared in wide circles about the Great Wizard, who was still a snake.

But Nischergurgje took the form of an eagle. He rose swiftly in the air. He overtook the Wicked Schlipme, and sank his claws into his back. He brought him down to earth.

Then Wicked Schlipme, bleeding and torn, howled:

"Now you have taken all my strength!"

And he sank down, down, into the dark Under Earth Land.

Nischergurgje went back to beat his Magic Drum and to cook his supper of reindeer flesh.

While over his head, across the deep dark sky, flashed and shimmered the many colored Northern Lights red, orange, yellow, green, blue, and violet. And the little brown Children of Lapland cried out:

"See! The warriors are fighting!"

KARI WOODENCOAT

BOOM! BOOM! BOOM! BEAT! BEAT! BEAT!
Listen to Nischergurgje!

A King had a son, and he had a kitchen girl. Her coat was made of three wooden boards.

One Sunday came, and Kari Woodencoat carried the washwater in to the King's Son. As she was shutting the door, the King's Son threw some drops of water at her.

When everyone was ready to go to Church, Kari Woodencoat said:

"May I go to Church?"

"NO! Stay in the kitchen and mind the dinner."

The Cook was afraid that Kari Woodencoat might start for Church, so she emptied a cask of grain on the ground. Kari Woodencoat must pick up every kernel!

She called the little birds to help, and they picked up the grain.

Then she dressed, and went to Church. She had a horse with a copper rein. Just when the Pastor said Amen, she went out, the King's Son after her. He asked her where she came from.

"From Washbasin Land!"

Sunday came again. Then Kari Woodencoat took the hand-towel in to the King's Son. She was closing the door, the King's Son threw the hand-towel at her.

The King's Son again went to Church. Kari Woodencoat asked whether she might go to Church.

"NO! Stay in the kitchen and cook the dinner."

The Cook emptied a cask of grain on the ground. Kari Woodencoat must pick up every bit of grain from the cask!

She called the little birds to help, and they picked up the grain.

Then she dressed herself for Church. Her horse had a silver rein, and her dress was clasped with silver clasps.

When she came to the Church, the King's Son had no time to listen to the Pastor's sermon. He looked at the girl. Just as the Pastor said Amen, Kari Woodencoat went out, the King's Son after her. He could not stop her. She climbed into the carriage and whipped up the horse.

Then the King's Son called:

"Where do you come from?"

"From Hand-towel Land!"

When the people got back from Church, there was Kari Woodencoat clattering around the kitchen in her wooden boards.

The third Sunday came. Kari Woodencoat took the comb in to the King's Son. Just as she closed the door, the King's Son opened the door and threw the comb at her.

It was again Church time. All were starting for Church, even the Cook. Then Kari Woodencoat said:

"May I go, too?"

"NO." She must stay in the kitchen and mind the dinner!

The Cook emptied a cask of grain. Kari Woodencoat must pick up the grain.

Then she called her little birds to help, and went to dress herself. Her horse had a golden rein. And she herself had golden clothes, and golden shoes on her feet.

When she went into the Church, the Church lighted up. There she was dressed all in gold!

The Pastor said Amen, and the golden girl went out, the King's Son after her.

He reached for her feet before she could climb into the carriage. A golden shoe was drawn off her foot.

The King's Son asked her from where she came.

"From Comb Land!"

When the people got home, there was Kari Woodencoat in the kitchen, dressed in her three wooden boards.

Then the King's Son made his father write to all kingdoms, to ask if Washbasin Land was anywhere.

NO!

Then he wrote to ask if Hand-towel Land as anywhere.

NO!

Then he wrote to see if Comb Land was anywhere.

It was not to be found.

Then he got together all the women to try on the golden shoe. But it fitted none of them. So small a foot the golden shoe fitted!

The Cook chopped off her toes and her heel, and tried on the golden shoe.

Then the little birds flew by, and called:

The toes chopped off!
The heel sliced off!
And the golden shoe full of blood!

Then the Cook cried out:

"If I had those birds here, I would chop them!"

After that Kari Woodencoat had to try on the golden shoe.

It fitted Kari Woodencoat!

THE GIANT WHO DID NOT LIKE BONES

BOOM! BOOM! BOOM! BEAT! BEAT! BEAT!
Listen to the Magic Drum!

Once upon a time, some Lapp children, without their parents knowing it, climbed into a boat and rowed out on a lake.

Now near this lake, in a great mountain cave, a Giant had his dwelling. He was not an ordinary Giant, but a Man-Eating Stallo. The children knew nothing of this. But the Giant learned somehow that the children were rowing on the lake, so he hurried to the shore and hid behind a big stone.

He began to call the children. They had never heard of him, so they thought it was their parents calling. They rowed hard to the shore. In a twinkling, just as the boat touched the land, up popped the Giant, lifted the boat to his shoulder, and hurried homeward. All this happened before the children could even think of running way.

The Giant was so tall that his shoulder brushed the highest branches of the trees. And the children, one after the other, caught hold of the branches and pulled themselves into the trees. Now the danger of their being eaten was over!

When the Giant reached his cave, he called out to his wife:

"Here! Choose two of these fat children, and prepare me a delicious feast."

"But you have brought only two," said the Giantess.

"Are you crazy?" cried the Giant, rumbling with anger.

27

But when he looked into the boat, he found only a little boy and a tiny girl, brother and sister. And they were so thin! Just skin and bones! Before they could be eaten, they had to be fattened.

Now the two little ones were put into a wooden pen. The Giantess brought them the most delicious food, roasted and baked, on gold and silver dishes, and ordered them to eat. But the boy understood what that meant. He told his sister not to touch the best-looking food, and to eat only enough to keep alive.

After a time, a guest came to see the Giant. The Giant wished, as is natural, to treat his guest to a tid-bit, so he went down to the pen where the children were. But when he found them scrawny and bony he was filled with rage.

"This boy here is as thin as a crow, and the girl is worse!" he exclaimed.

Then he slung both children on his back, and carried them to their parents' hut. He threw them inside, roaring out:

"Here! Take your miserable young ones! Such bony skeletons, I will not have!"

And back he ran to his dwelling, so that the earth shook under his feet.

NAUGHTY, NAUGHTY SPIDER!

BUZZ! Buzz! Buzz! Listen to the swarming gnats!

In Lapland when the summer sun burns hot, day and night, the Lapp children have much pain. This is all because of the spider!

In old days there were no mosquitoes in Lapland. But in the pleasant country to the south, the mosquitoes lived, and buzzed, and sucked their suppers.

One day all the mosquitoes began to talk of seeing Lapland, for they had heard so much about it. A spider, that had run about Lapland, had told them of its wonders. How the cuckoos sang sweetly, the berries ripened, and the flowers bloomed! Yes indeed! And the reindeer had such juicy skins, and there were dogs and goats and little animals with no places to hide in; and Lapp children sleeping outside without covers. And there were nice wet bogs waiting for the mosquitoes' eggs. And the sun shone night and day, so that the mosquitoes could always find food.

But that spider did not tell them of the long, freezing night, when the sun never shone for weeks! Nor did the spider say:

"Such fine nets as I spin among the loose stones, where mosquitoes do not see them!"

Oh yes! Those southern mosquitoes longed to be in Lapland. But the Mother of the Mosquitoes said:

"First let us send some scouts there, to find what the land is like."

Six went. A reindeer whisked one of them off his tail and crushed it. Another fell into a milking pail and was drowned. The third was smothered by tent-smoke. A fourth was killed by an old Lapp woman. Only two got safely back to the pleasant southern land.

These two said that Lapland was good in spots.

The Mother of the Mosquitoes then said:

"Let the gnats go to Lapland. We will stay here."

But the two scout mosquitoes said, that everything would be well if all the mosquitoes together, at once, would fly north. So all the mosquitoes in a great swarm flew north to Lapland.

Oh yes! There they are today, when the summer sun burns hot—swarms and swarms of them, like dark clouds. They buzz and bite.

Oh yes! And the spider spins and spins and spins fine nets among the loose stones, where the mosquitoes cannot see them. The mosquitoes fly into the nets, and the spider runs along the threads and eats them!

WHAT HAPPENED TO SOME
LAPP CHILDREN

BOOM! BOOM! BOOM! BEAT! BEAT! BEAT!
Listen to Nischergurgje!

THE BOYS WHO DID NOT GET
A MAGIC COW

ONCE on a time in Lapland of the Northern Lights, where the rich Lapp Kings own great herds of reindeer—pack reindeer, mother reindeer, and pretty little fawns—once on a time on a summer's day when the sun was shining hot, a Lapp King with his whole company of Lapps drove a reindeer herd into a green valley to graze.

The men unharnessed the pack reindeer, took off their burdens, and set up tents close to a rock. The women hung cooking pots over the fire, and began to boil reindeer meat.

None of these Lapps knew that their camp was pitched near the place of sacrifice to a Seite. This Seite was a huge ugly stone, of strange and fearful shape.

The Seite belonged to a Lapland Wizard. Whenever he wanted to get magic power and have wicked spirits help him to put evil on someone, he chose a fine white reindeer-buck out of his herd, and decorated it. Every part he decorated—antlers, head, legs, back—with yellow, blue, green, red-brown, white, and black silk.

When the buck was ready it knew just where to go. It led the way to the Seite, and the Wizard followed. There the Wizard killed the buck, ate its flesh, and cast its bones and horns on a huge pile of reindeer bones and antlers near the Seite. In this way he got all the magic power he wanted, to bring revenge on his enemies.

So near this spot the Lapp company camped with their reindeer herd. Now in the Lapp King's tent were two Lapp boys. Night came on though the sun still shone, for it never set night or day at that time of the year. The two Lapp boys, for some strange cause, could not sleep. By and by they heard Voices in the rocks. They knew then, that those rocks were the home of some Ulda Fairy Folk.

The boys peeped out of the tent. They saw a whole herd of Ulda magic reindeer cows grazing. They were white and had no horns.

The boys knew that if they threw a piece of steel over the herd, they could keep a cow for themselves. That would bring good luck and riches! But before they could throw it, the reindeer vanished.

THE ULDAS' OLD MOTHER

Now this is what happened once, in Lapland of the Northern Lights!

The Lapps know that Ulda Fairy Folk carry off children, so Lapp fathers and mothers give their children amulets of silver, brass, or copper, to frighten away the Uldas.

There was once a Lapp Mother, who did not give her baby an amulet. One day she saw that her child was looking funny, and acting funnily.

She knew then that the Uldas had carried off her own child, and had left a changeling.

An old Lapp woman told her:

"You must whip that changeling hard. You must put it in a room by itself"—for the Lapp Mother lived in a house—"and you must set a small plate of porridge on the table, with many spoons. Then see what you shall see!

The Lapp Mother did this. She shut the child in a room with a tiny dish of porridge and many spoons. Then she heard the child say:

I've lived as long as the dwarf birches,
Lived as long as mountain birches,
Never have I seen such doings!
Many spoons and little porridge

Then the Lapp Mother knew for sure, that the child was a changeling. She rushed in and whipped it hard—whipped, and whipped, and whipped—beat, and beat, and beat! Then she locked the changeling in by itself, but first she set some burning lights in the room.

By and by she heard Voices. The Uldas were speaking.

"They have been beating our Old Mother," said the Voices. "We cannot stand that!"

And when the Lapp Mother opened the door and peeped in, there was her own child safe and sound. The Uldas had carried off their Old Mother!

You may be sure that the Lapp Mother, as quick as she could, gave her child a silver amulet. She put a knife in its cradle, and fastened silver buttons and other amulets to the three-stringed band that hung from the top of the cradle to its foot.

That frightened away the Uldas.

THE MOON DAUGHTER'S MAGIC

BOOM! BOOM! BOOM! BEAT! BEAT! BEAT!
Listen to Nischergurgje's Magic Drum!

Far back in the ages when the woodcock was white and the blackbird was gray, and before there were any mosquitoes and gnats, in Lapland lived two mighty Wizards. One was named Torajas and the other Karkias.

Each had his own hunting ground, and his own place to graze his reindeer herd. A wide lake lay between the dwellings of the two.

They were great Wizards, these two, for Tonto the Spirit of the Magic Drum had given them some of his power. He had taught them many Spells, and how to say them backward to undo the Spells. The two could race invisible like the Storm Wind through the skN. They could fly like dipping, soaring eagles. They could become serpents. And in the forms of fleet reindeer with broad antlers, they could skim over the snow-slopes. All they had to do, was to beat their Magic Drums, chant their Spells, and become what they willed.

Karkias had only good signs painted on the drum-head of his Magic Drum. He never used his skill to harm any human being.

But Torajas had on his drum, not only the good signs Great Nischergurgje had taught the Lapland Wizards, but also the evil signs of Black Magic learned from Schlipme, Wicked Wizard of the Wicked Moon Daughter.

Things were going well with the little brown men of Lapland. Their fat herds of tame reindeer were increasing. Their hunting and fishing were good. They often went to Karkias to ask his aid. They were very rich and happy.

Now down in the dark, dank Underworld, sat the hideous Wicked Moon Daughter. Her hair, coarse and stringy, fell over her caved-in-forehead. Her long yellow teeth gleamed in her crooked mouth. She gnashed her teeth with rage, because the little brown men were happy.

Quickly she changed herself into a Blackbird, and flew to the tent of Torajas. She perched on a pine tree near his door, and sang:

Lapland's Wizards, they are mighty!
Two are famed for skill and Magic.
Torajas beats his Dram with cunning.
Marked with Black Art's signs, his Drum is.
Karkias is wise and powerful,
Filled he is with age-old Magic,
Great his Spells and his enchantments.
Which is greater, which more powerful,
Karkias, or strong Torajas?
So the Lapland people wonder!

Thus sang the Wicked Moon Daughter in the shape of a bird. The proud Torajas heard her, and began to wonder in his heart whether Karkias knew more Spells than he did, or had as many signs painted on his Drum, as he, Torajas, had on his.

Looking into Torajas' heart, the Wicked Moon Daughter saw that her song had moved him to envy. She flapped her black bat-like wings, and flew down and sat by his door, and sang:

Let the Lapland people find out
Which of you is greater Wizard.
Let a trial be between you,
Let the winner be Chief Wizard!

At this Torajas' heart was moved with badness. And the huge Blackbird, flapping her wings, flew croaking back to her dark home in the Under Earth Land.

Her song still rang in Torajas' ears. Hateful thoughts drove all joy from him. The darkness of the Underworld began to spread in his heart. Envy and bitterness against the good Wizard Karkias were rooted in his mind.

Through long days, did hatred grow stronger in his heart.

One morning he stood by the lake and saw the good Wizard rowing a raft on the water. Torajas muttered a Spell, and straightway the storm spirits came rushing over the lake lashing the billows sky high.

Before Karkias could speak a single Magic Word, the wind lifted the frail raft, and tossed it into the air. Karkias fell to the bottom of the lake.

He changed himself into a small, swift fish, and began to swim towards land. But Torajas muttered another Spell and sent a huge pike that lived in the lake, to devour Karkias. The pike swallowed him down whole.

Then all the Lapland people missed Karkias, and said:

"Surely he was the great Nischergurgje himself, and has vanished. Karkias is the greatest of all Wizards!"

Twelve months went by. Often around the tent of the bad Wizard, Torajas, flew the huge Blackbird, singing:

Which is greater here in Lapland,
Karkias the vanished Wizard,
Or the fearless one, Torajas?

Then Torajas' heart became all evil. Chanting songs of Black Magic, he went to set his net in the lake. The next day, when he drew the net, it was full of little fishes. The next day he set the net across the whole lake. When he drew it in the morning, it was full of larger fishes.

Then he called on the Wicked Moon Daughter for help and sank his net. And see! The next morning when he pulled it, the huge pike was in the middle of it.

Torajas took up the pike, and carried it to the Lapland folk. Standing among them, he plunged his knife into the pike. Of course he thought to kill it. See! Out stept Karkias well and whole.

"Evil Torajas!" he cried. "You did wrong to use Black Magic against me."

When the Lapland people heard this, they exclaimed:

"Torajas is a bad Wizard. We will have nothing to do with him. Karkias is the greatest Wizard in Lapland."

Raging and fuming, Torajas went back to his side of the lake. And after that no one ever asked him for help.

But the Wicked Moon Daughter stayed about his tent. And every time she flapped her black wings, stinging mosquitoes and buzzing biting gnats filled the air.

THE RED-HAIRED WIZARD

BOOM! BOOM! BOOM! BEAT! BEAT! BEAT!—
BOOM! BOOM! BOOM! through the long Arctic Night and
across the white snow plains!

So ended the Great Nischergurgje his stories.

And the Four Ancient Wizards of the South Baltic Lands, ground their teeth, whistled, howled, and were still.

And as Nischergurgie beat! beat! beat! on is Magic Drum and tapped! tapped! tapped! on his Magic Drum, all Lapland was silent. The stars shone big in the dark winter sky. From the edge of the world sprang up the Northern Lights like a tent of colored flames—red, orange, yellow, green, blue, and violet. The colored flames darted here, darted there, shifted, wavered, and spread to and fro over the sky.

And the Lapp children slid about swiftly on their skis and shouted mockingly:

"Northern Lights, flicker! Flicker! Flicker!"

Then the children, scared and trembling, ran into the tents to hide, crying out:

"Northern Lights, do not take our eyes!"

And a great silence fell upon the Four Ancient Wizards, and upon the Lapp tents. The dwarf birches, in their veils of filigree crystals, sparkled like rainbows. Threads of hoar frost and glittering ice lay on the eyebrows and hair of the Four Ancient Wizards, as they sat on the snow in front of the Great Nischergurgje.

39

Oh, very, very cold it was! The smoke, from the smoke-holes of the Lapp tents, curled straight up through the biting air. A flock of little birds, like snowflakes, settled down on dwarf birch and aspen.

"Great Comrades!" cried Nischergurgje. "See! The little snow-buntings come flocking down from the mountains; it bodes a storm of snow. See! The Northern Lights flash quickly; it bodes a fierce, high wind. See! Northern Lights spread widely; it bodes a deep, deep, heaping snow. See! The Northern Lights are many; it bodes a freezing, howling wind from the Pole.

"Your boots are stuffed with warm, sweet hay, and your robes are wrapped closely around you, yet not all your Magic will keep you warm! Come then, let us sit around yonder Lapp fire."

So into the biggest Lapp tent went Nischergurgje and the Four Ancient Wizards and sat them down on the birch boughs spread on the floor. And in the narrow space around the blazing smoking fire, they sat between Lapp children, Lapp men, and the little dogs.

And the Lapp women brought a feast—tasty morsels of reindeer flesh, hot from the cooking pot over the fire, reindeer marrow-bones, reindeer cheese in wooden saucers, reindeer milk mixed with dried berries, fragrant coffee with lumps of sugar and frozen reindeer milk, drinks of melted snow water, and tiny rye cakes baked before the fire.

Boom! Boom! Boom! The feast was over.

And the Great Nischergurgje struck his Drum with his golden hammer, and cried out:

"Kauko, Red-Haired Wizard of Finland, tell us Wonder Tales from your Thousand Lakes and Thousand Isles."

And the Four Ancient Wizards whistled, ground their teeth, howled, and were still.

And all the Lapp people were still.

Kauko the Red-Haired Wizard laid aside his own Drum.

He took up his living speaking Kantele, and drew his hand across its strings. Wild and weird was his music.

Then Kauko the Red-Haired Wizard began his stories.

CLING! CLING! CLING! CLANG! CLING!

FROM FINLAND OF
THE THOUSAND LAKES LOST
DAUGHTER OF THE BALTIC SEA

Where the lovely lilies tremble,
Golden lilies on the waters;
Where the fir tree points its candles,
Points its slender spire towards Heaven;
And the streams make mighty music,
From the rocks in cascades foaming—
There dwells Finland's Baltic Wizard,
There he makes his Tales of Wonder.
Welds them on his Forge of Magic,
Beats them with his Magic Hammer.

They are wrought from Songs of Magic,
Songs of ancient Vainamoinen,
Finland's vanished sweet-tongued Wizard,
Wrought from Runes of Vainamoinen;
Till they live and leap and quiver,
Till they shout with songs and laughter,
Till they weep with tears of woman,
Till they stir the heart with pity.
So makes Finland's Baltic Wizard
All his Tales of Magic Wonder;
Beats them on his Forge of Magic,
Beats them with his Magic Hammer.

MAGIC SINGING

CLING! CLING! CLING! CLANG! CLING!
Listen to the Red-Haired Wizard from the Land of a
Thousand Lakes!

In the days of Golden Wonders, when the world was made from an egg—the earth from its lower half, the sky from its upper part, the moonshine from its white, and the sunshine from its yellow—the great, ancient Wizard Vainamoinen came to the Land of Heroes.

Out of the rolling, tossing billows, out of the white-wreathed waves, out of the crested seafoam, crept that wonderful enchanter. He stood up on a wide and desolate isle. Then he called a Magic Youth and bade him sow seed of many kinds. The Magic Youth sowed seed on swamp and lowland, on mountain and hill. Fir trees sprang up on the mountains, pine trees on the hills, slender birches in the swamps, and lindens in the valleys. And junipers grew up, all hung with clustering berries.

Not only on that isle, but in the Land of Heroes spread wide, wide forests and meadows. Merry thrushes sang among the forest trees, and velvet-throated cuckoos trilled in the silver birches. Luscious strawberries and cloudberries nestled among their own leaves. Golden flowers grew on the meads. Lovely was the Land of Heroes!

Then the ancient, wise Vainamoinen, with his Belt full of Wonder Tales, passed his days happily in the Land of Heroes. Far, far away sounded his voice. All the people in the South Lands heard his Magic Songs and Tales, and even the folk of far Lapland listened in wonder to them.

Now in far dismal Lapland dwelt a young Wizard, Youkahainen by name. He heard the Lapland folk say:

"The sweet Singer of the Land of Heroes, is better skilled in Tales and Magic than is our Youkahainen."

At that minute, black envy entered Youkahainen's heart.

"I will go to the Land of Heroes!" exclaimed he. "I will challenge this ridiculous Wizard to a contest. I will sing him my oldest Tales and chant my powerful Magic Words. I will put him to shame, and transform him into some mean thing. He shall sing the worst of songs."

Then Youkahainen rushed to his stable and led out his horse. Flames darted from its nostrils. Sparks flew from under its hoofs. Youkahainen hitched his horse to a golden sledge, and, leaping on the sledge, took his dog beside him. He struck the horse with his pearl decorated birch-whip. Away they sped with thunderous clatter. All that day the horse galloped southward, all the next day, onward and onward. On the third day, Youkahainen reached the heath-covered meadow in the Land of Heroes, where Vainamoinen dwelt.

Now it happened that the ancient Vainamoinen himself, driving his own golden sledge, came racing along the roadway. Youkahainen saw him coming, and did not turn out. Fiercely he urged on his foaming horse, and dashed upon Vainamoinen. The two sledges struck. Their shafts were driven together. The reins and traces were tangled. The two horses stood still, smoking and fiery.

"Who are you, and whence come you?" cried the ancient Vainamoinen. "You drive like a silly boy. You have broken my sledge and ruined my reins and traces."

"I am the young and wise Lapland Wizard," sneered Youkahainen. "What low fellow are you, and where do you come from? Is it possible that you are the famous Wizard and Singer, Vainamoinen? If so, let us sing together. Let us chant our Magic Songs. He who is the sweetest Singer shall keep the roadway. The other shall take the roadside."

"I accept your challenge," said the ancient Vainamoinen. "But first tell me, golden youngster, some of the wisest things you know."

"O my wisdom is great indeed! I know many wise things," answered Youkahainen. "Listen!"

Every roof must have a chimney,
Every fireplace a hearthstone.
Lives of seals are free and merry.
Salmon eat the perch and whiting.
Lapps still plow the land with reindeer.
In your land they plow with horses.
This is some of my great wisdom!

"Such foolish stuff," said the ancient Vainamoinen, "may suit women and babes, but not bearded heroes. Tell me, now, what happened when the world began?"

"O well, I know much wisdom about that too!" boasted Youkahainen. "Listen!"

Boiling water is malicious.
Fire is very full of danger.
Magic is the child of seafoam.
Waters gush from every mountain.
Fir trees were the first of houses;
Hollow stones, the first of kettles.

"Foolish words!" cried Vainamoinen. "Is that all the nonsense you can talk?"

"O I can tell you what really happened in those golden first days," said Youkahainen. "Listen!"

For 'twas I who plowed the ocean;
Hollowed out the depths of ocean;
When I dug the salmon grottoes,
When I all the lakes created,
When I heaped the mountains round them,
When I piled the rocks around them.
I was present as a hero,
When, the heavens were created,
When the sky was crystal-pillared,
When was arched the beauteous rainbow,
When the silver sun was planted,
And with stars the heavens were sprinkled.

"You are a shameless liar!" cried Vainamoinen. "The Prince of all liars!"

"Come, you old Wizard!" shouted Youkahainen, tossing back his black hair. "Let us fight with knives! If you are afraid to fight, why then I will sing you into a wild boar of the forest, with swinish snout and swinish heart!"

At that Vainamoinen waxed fierce with rage. He frowned terribly. Then he began his Magic Singing, began his Magic Incantations. Grandly sang the wise Vainamoinen, sang till the mountains shook with fear and the flinty rocks and ledges heard his Magic Tones and crumbled, and the billows heaved and thundered on the shore.

And the boastful Youkahainen stood still in terror. Vainamoinen sang and sang, and he changed Youkahainen's sledge-runners into saplings; sang his reins into alders; sang the golden sledge to float upon a lake; changed the birch-whip, pearl-ornamented, into a reed, and the horse into a white stone by the water.

And the grand old Vainamoinen sang and sang; sang Youkahainen's gold-handled dagger into a gleam of lightning in the sky above him; his painted crossbow into a rainbow; his feathered arrows into hawks

48

soaring around his head; his dog into a block of stone; sang his cap off his forehead, sang it into wreaths of white vapor; sang his gloves into waterlilies, and his belt set with jewels into a twinkling band of stars around him.

And as Vainamoinen sang and sang, Youkahainen began to sink into a swamp of mud and water; he sank and sank to his waist. He could not lift his feet, and great pains shot through him.

"O wise Vainamoinen!" he cried in terror. "O you greatest of all Wizards! Speak your Magic Words backwards, repeat your Magic Incantation backwards, and free me from this place of horror. I will pay you a rich ransom."

"What ransom will you give me," asked Vainamoinen, "if I will cease my Enchantments, if I will turn away my Magic?"

"Free me from this torment," cried Youkahainen, "and I will give you my two Magic Crossbows that hang in my Lapland house."

"I do not wish your Magic Crossbows. I have bows banging on every nail and rafter."

Then Vainamoinen sang again, and poor Youkahainen sank deeper and deeper in the mud and water.

"Oh, I will give you my Magic Boats, swift, beautiful, and wonderful!"

"I do not want your Magic Boats. My bays are full of Wonder Boats."

Then Vainamoinen sang poor Youkahainen deeper, deeper, and yet deeper into the mud and water, till he cried in anguish:

"I will give you my Magic Horses!"

"I do not want your Magic Horses. Magic Horses crowd my stables."

Deeper, deeper, down, down, down, sank poor Youkahainen to his shoulders, and he offered gold that glitters in the sunshine and silver that gleams in the moonshine, and all his cornfields and his corn. But sorrow laden and enchanted, he sank to his chin in the mud and water. Seaweed filled his nostrils and grass tangled in his teeth.

"O, you ancient Vainamoinen!" prayed and beseeched poor Youkahainen. "Wisest of all wisdom-singers! Stop your Magic Incantations. Turn away your Magic Spells. Save me from this smothering torment. Free my eyes from sand and torture. I will give you my Sister Aino. Fairest of all LaplandÕs daughters! She shall be your bride, sweep your rooms and keep your house. She shall rinse your golden platters, and weave golden covers for your bed. She shall bake your honey-biscuit."

"That is the ransom I wish!" exclaimed the ancient Vainamoinen. "Lapland's young and fairest daughter to be my lovely bride forever, and the pride of the Land of Heroes!"

Then joyfully Vainamoinen sat down upon a rock, and sang a little, then sang again, then sang a third time. Backwards he weaved his Magic Incantations and backwards sang his Magic Songs. The charm was broken!

Youkahainen dragged his feet from the mud, lifted his chin from out of the mud, and stood up. He led his horse away from the water, drew his golden sledge to land, picked up his pearl ornamented birch-whip, hitched his horse to his sledge, threw himself on the sledge, and snapped his whip. Heavy-hearted and sorrowful he sped away to Lapland.

Night and day the horse galloped, and on the third day Youkahainen reached his home. He drove recklessly against the house-wall, broke his shafts, and smashed his golden sledge.

His Mother, gray and aged, came running out to meet him.

"Why do you break your snow-sledge, son?" cried his Father. "Why do you come home in this wild way?"

Then poor Youkahainen wept, broken-hearted.

"Tell me, First-born, why do you weep?" asked his Mother.

"Golden Mother, ever faithful!" cried Youkahainen. "Surely I have cause to weep. I have promised my dearest Sister, your beloved Aino, to the ancient Wizard Vainamoinen, to be his bride."

Then his Mother clapped her hands with joy. But the fair and darling Maiden, the beautiful Aino, fell to bitter weeping.

"Now listen all ye Lapp People," cried the Red-Haired Wizard of the Land of a Thousand Lakes.

Soon I'll tell you more of Aino,
And of Vainamoinen's wooing;
And more of Lapland's Rainbow Maiden,
And the Wondrous Magic Sampo.

THE LIVING KANTELE

RING! RING! SING! SING!
Listen to Kauko the Red-Haired Wizard,
as he plays on his living Kantele!

A widow had a son, who lived with his Mother. One day he said to her:

"I will go out into the world to earn money."

But the Mother said, "Why would you go away? Buy yourself a gun and dog, and hunt in the wood."

So he bought himself a gun and dog and went into the wood. He wandered about the whole day, wandered about the wood, and found nothing. Vexed, he returned home, and said to his Mother:

"You wanted me to buy a gun and a dog, and I have got nothing by it."

His Mother said, "You must learn to hunt for many days."

The next day he went out again into the wood, but shot nothing.

He did not wish to go to the wood any more, but his Mother made him go. On the third day, the dog barked at a squirrel in a tree. He was just going to shoot it, when the squirrel spoke.

"Do not shoot me," it said. "I will come down."

So he did not shoot it, and the squirrel crept down the pine tree, down, down, then leaped to the ground in front of the lad.

It turned into a Maiden, such a beautiful Maiden that the lad could not keep his eyes off her.

The Maiden said, "Because you have not shot me, I will be your bride."

"You are beautiful and please me," said he, "but I do not dare to do it. What would my Mother say?"

"Just take me to your Mother," said she, "and if she lets you, why marry me. If she does not, I will go back to the wood."

So he took her home, and the Maiden stayed out in the courtyard while the lad went in and said to his Mother:

"There is such a lovely and good Maiden, that I want for my bride, if you will say yes."

So his Mother gave her permission, and he took the Maiden for his bride. She was most beautiful, and they lived happily together.

Now the Emperor's Son had been searching three whole years for a bride, but could not find one that pleased him. When he saw the lad's bride he wanted very much to have her for his own.

Then he thought, "Well, I cannot take her from a living husband!" Then he went to the lad's house, and said, "To-night, you must build me over yonder rapids, a golden bridge with silver railings."

The lad was troubled and went to his wife. She asked:

"Why are you so sad?"

"To-night I must build for the Emperor's Son a golden bridge with silver railings."

"Lie down and go to sleep," said his wife. "We will think it over to-night."

After she had thought about it, she gave her beloved a silken handkerchief, saying:

"Go now, strike the water of the rapids with this cloth. Say at the same time, To-night a golden bridge with silver railings shall stand here."

Then he struck the water with the handkerchief, and said this. He went to sleep and slept the night through. And in the morning the bridge was finished.

The Emperor's Son came and stared.

"O well, it is much nicer than we hoped!"

Then he set the lad another task. He said to him:

"In the garden here, are buried three golden piglets. They must be found to-night. If you do not find them, I will cut off your head."

Again the lad went with a troubled mind to his wife, and she asked:

"Why are you so sad?"

"To-night I must produce three golden piglets that are buried in the garden."

"Lie down and go to sleep. We will think it over to-night, how to get them."

They slept the whole night through. The next morning said she:

"Go to the Emperor's Son. Take with you to the garden the Highest General and a spade. In the midst of the garden, stands an oak. Under it dig a pit three fathoms deep. In it you will find the three piglets close to each other."

That he did, and found the three piglets close to each other. He lifted them out.

"There they are!"

After that he went back to his house and his wife.

The Emperor's Son, however, was very much provoked, and he set him another task.

"Now you shall procure for me a Living Kantele, that plays by itself. If you do not get just such a living Kantele, then I will cut off your head."

Again the lad went troubled to his wife, and she asked:

"Why are you so sad?"

"I must procure a Kantele, a Living Kantele, that plays by itself."

Then answered his wife:

"Go to the Emperor, and demand of him three of the Highest Generals. Then come back to me, that I may send you where you will procure the Living Kantele," said his wife.

Soon he came back to his wife with the Generals, and she gave her beloved another Silken Handkerchief and a Blue Ball of thread. Then she charged him to demand of the Emperor three months and a day in which to fetch the Kantele. And the Emperor gave him this respite.

Just as they were starting on their way, his wife said to him:

"In whatever direction I throw this Ball, follow it. Then you shall find the self-playing Kantele. After you leave here, show this Handkerchief at two places. But do not show it a third time, till you are in the most dreadful of difficulties."

They started out. The Blue Ball rolled and rolled before him; and the three Generals and the Son of the Widow followed it.

They travelled on, and came to a little hut that was covered with earth, like a charcoal burner's hut.

They went inside, and there was an Old Woman sitting in a rocking-chair. She said:

"Oho! For thirty years I have not smelled a human being. Now here comes a roast for my supper!"

But the lad said, "What? You are my Aunt, and would you eat us for supper?"

Then he fetched his Silken Handkerchief out of his pocket, and wiped his face with it. At that muttered she:

"Ah! That is my son-in-law, the husband of my daughter!"

Then he must have something to eat and drink, and she did not know how to treat him well enough!

That night they stayed there, and the next morning they started out. The Ball ran before them along the highway.

Again they came to a hut that looked like a charcoal burner's hut. The Blue Ball ran into the hut. There sat an Old Woman in a rocking-chair, just like the first, only older.

"Oho!" said she. "For sixty years I have not smelled a human being. Now here comes a roast for my supper!"

"What? Will you eat me, a traveller, you who are my Aunt?"

He again took out the Handkerchief and wiped his face.

"Aha!" said she. "That is my nephew, the husband of my niece!"

He was entertained, and stayed the night there. They all got fine food and drink.

When morning dawned, the Blue Ball rolled again before them along the highway.

It ran and it ran, and then it came to a third hut, like the others. They went in, and there sat a yet older Old Woman in a rocking-chair. She spoke:

"Oho! For ninety years I have smelled no human beings. Now I am getting something for supper!"

The lad said, "Why would you eat us, who are travellers? The flesh of a traveller is like gristle, and the soup of him tastes like washwater."

Then they ate and drank out of their own knapsack, and the Son of the Widow spoke:

"We are searching for a Living Kantele. Who can make us one?"

The Old Woman answered:

"Hi! my Boys can make it, but they are in the forest. They will not come home till twilight."

"O well! If they are coming, why we will wait for them."

They waited the whole evening till it was dark. Then three wolves sprang into the hut, leaped over the rafters, and jumped from the dresser, and turned themselves into three handsome young men.

They began to make the Living Kantele, and they told one of the Generals to hold the pine-board.

"If you fall asleep," said they, "it will not go well with you!"

Then they worked on the Kantele. The General held the board, fell asleep, and snored. As he slept, they turned themselves into wolves, gobbled him up for their supper, and ran out into the forest.

The Old Woman said, "They will not come home again till evening."

The lad waited till evening. As it was growing dark, again the three wolves sprang into the hut, leaped from the dresser, and became men.

56

Again they began to work on the Kantele, and told the second General to hold the board.

"If you sleep, something will happen, as you saw by the other one!"

The General held the pine-board, fell asleep, and snored.

The young men turned themselves again into wolves, gobbled him for their supper, and ran howling into the forest.

"They will not come home before evening," said the Old Woman again.

"All right! When they come, the Kantele must be finished."

They all spent the day walking in the forest, and evening came again. Once more the three wolves sprang into the hut, leaped from the dresser, and turned themselves into men. Now must the last General hold the board! And they said to him:

"Do not you dare to sleep! If you sleep, nothing good will happen!"

He held the board, held it and was a little bit sleepy. He tried hard not to fall asleep, but soon he was snoring. Immediately the young men turned themselves into wolves, and gobbled up the last General.

The lad was alone with the Old Woman!

"They will not come back again before evening."

"All right! When they come, the Kantele must be finished."

Twilight fell. Came the wolves, leaped from the dresser, and changed into men. They began to work on the Living Kantele, and it was the Son of the Widow, who must hold the board this time!

He held it, and held it, became tired, and the young men poked him in the side.

"What? Are you asleep?"

"NO! I am not asleep. I am wondering whether there is more dry than fresh wood in the forest?"

Then they changed themselves into wolves.

"Wait! We will count, and see whether there is more dry or more fresh wood in the forest?"

There they counted the whole day through till evening, then back they came. Again sprang the three wolves over the rafters, down from the dresser, and became men. They worked at the Kantele, and the lad held the board.

He held it, and held it, and grew sleepy. Then he took out the Silken Handkerchief and wiped his eyes. The Old Woman saw it.

"Ah!" said she. "That is the husband of my niece! Why did you not tell me before? The Kantele would have been finished long ago."

Then she entertained him. While she was preparing the food, the young men finished the Kantele.

When the Kantele was all ready, their Mother said to the young men:

"Turn yourselves into wolves. Take him on your backs, and carry him home as quickly as you can, before the Emperor's Son steals his bride."

Then they took him on their backs, and he rode with the most terrible swiftness.

Already the Emperor's Son had carried off the bride to his house, and was going to hold the wedding. The lad threw the Living Kantele down before him.

"Here is the Kantele. Why did you take my bride away before my promised time was up?"

And he rescued his bride from the Emperor's Son, and brought her to his Mother. And they are living there to this very day.

THE HIDDEN MAIDEN

RING! RING! RING! RING!
Listen to the Living Speaking Kantele!

In the land where the sea shines white in the twilight of midnight, where the Kantele sighs and breathes the sweetest music, there stands an ancient Castle. Its frowning massive walls rise from an island. Around the walls flows a strong current of water, so deep that it looks inky black. Icy cold is the water and swift of current. There never was a swimmer who could swim through that current guarding the Castle.

Fiercely frowns the Castle, for it knows many a terrible secret. Its thick walls are silent, and they are blind for they have no outside windows.

Once, long ago, the brave Finns held the Castle against the attacking Russian foe. They were defending a lovely Swedish Maiden from the enemy who wished to seize her. At last, just as the Russians were taking the Castle, the girl's brave defenders hid her away in a secret place. With great difficulty the Russians scaled the walls. One by one, they killed the Finns. At last there was no one left to tell where the Maiden was.

The Russian soldiers entered the great hall, grand and gloomy, where the flare of torches fell upon the armor. But no Maiden was there. They rushed up the stairway, they searched the round tower, they climbed deep down into the hollow vaults, but the Maiden was not there. In vain they searched in every corner, room, and dungeon, the lovely Swedish Maiden was never found.

Time went by, high up on the wall an ash-tree, delicate and graceful, grew up out of the stones. Then men knew where the Maiden was. Her defenders, rather than let her fall into the hands of the foe, had sealed her close in the wall, where her shrieks and moans could not betray her. Then all had died defending her, and no one was left to tell where she was hidden.

And there the ash-tree hangs to-day. So rings and sings the sweet sad music of the Kantele!

THE RAINBOW MAIDEN

CLING! CLING! CLING! CLANG! CLING!
Listen to the Red-Haired Wizard from Suomi the beautiful of the
thousand lakes and thousand isles!

Listen to his tale of Vainamoinen, Ancient Wizard:

It was in those first Golden Wonder Days that the rash boastful
Youkahainen promised his lovely, young sister Aino to be the bride of
the Ancient Vainamoinen.

But Aino, weeping bitter tears, clad herself in the finest of blue robes,
adorned her head with gold and silver, girded herself with a golden girdle,
and tied bands of blue and scarlet about her forehead.

Then she wandered hither and yon; for three days she wandered,
singing sadly, singing madly, till on the third day she reached the purple
border of a blue lake. There she hung her silken robes on an alder, and
her scarlet and blue ribbands on an aspen. Down she sat on a large,
many-colored rock in the water, and wailed and lamented.

Then suddenly the rock sank to the bottom of the lake, and the lovely
Maiden Aino became a Water-Maiden in the grottoes of the Lake King.
Sometimes in the form of a water-salmon she swam to and fro in the
waves.

Now it happened that Vainamoinen heard of the wonder-salmon, and
set out to catch it. Day after day, in his copper boat, he glided over the
waves, but he fished in vain with his copper rod and golden line. Though
he caught the salmon once, it slipped through his fingers into the water.

Then Aino in her fish-shape raised her head above the waves, and cried mockingly:

"O Vainamoinen, pitiful old thing! You have not the wit to hold me! I am the darling of the Water King, the youngest Daughter of the Surge!"

Then turning away, she dived deep, deep into the lake, and was never seen again.

The ancient Vainamoinen, with bowed head and sorrowful sighs, guided his copper boat to land.

The days passed, and he was lonely and grief-stricken. Then thought he:

"I will go to dismal, distant Lapland, and there seek the Rainbow Maiden for my bride. She, the most beautiful of all Maidens, dwells upon a Magic Rainbow."

So to the land of cruel winter, the land of little sunshine, Vainamoinen, mounted on his Magic Dappled Steed, plunged onward, onward towards the cold Northern land. Still onward the Magic Dappled Steed galloped, till it reached the blue sea water. Then over the water it sped.

Now it happened that the boastful Youkahainen, Lapland's most wicked Wizard, saw Vainamoinen skimming over the blue waves. He raised his Magic Crossbow, drew its cruel bow-string, and loosed a feathered arrow. Fast sped the arrow, stuck the Magic Dappled Steed, and passed through Vainamoinen's shoulder. Headlong into the sea, plunged Vainamoinen.

Then the boastful evil Youkahainen thought that Vainamoinen was dead, so he hurried home boasting more loudly.

But the rolling billows upheld the ancient Wizard. He swam through the deep sea, and floated on the tide like a branch of aspen. He swam six days in summer, and six nights in golden moonlight. Then there rose a mighty Wind Storm, and an eagle came soaring around his head. On its back, the eagle carried him to the coast of dismal Lapland, set him down, and flew away.

Then Vainamoinen, old and lonely, sat down beside the border of the blue sea, and fell to bitter weeping. Three long days he wept and lamented.

Now it chanced that the Rainbow Maiden, rosy and beautiful, went out early one morning to gather six white fleeces from six gentle lambkins, to make her a robe of the softest raiment. She heard a wailing from the water, a weeping from the seashore, a hero's voice lamenting. Straight she ran to her mother, old Louhi the Lapland Witch.

Old Louhi, toothless creature, hurried down to the water-side. There she found Vainamoinen weeping in a grove of alders and shivering aspens. His locks were flowing wildly and his lips were trembling. She led him to her dwelling, fed him, let him warm himself at her fire, and then said:

"Weep no more, O Vainamoinen, Wizard Great of the Land of Heroes! Grieve no more, friend of the waters! Live here with us, and be always welcome. You shall eat salmon from our platters, feed on the sweetest of bacon and the most delicate of small fish."

But Vainamoinen answered shaking his head strangely:

"O Lapland Witch, I am grateful! Though toothsome and delicate is your food, yet food in my own home is more to me. It is better to dwell in my own beloved home in the Land of Heroes, there to drink cool, clear water in birchen cups, than in strange lands to quaff the richest liquor from golden bowls."

"What will you give me, O ancient Vainamoinen," said the Witch, "if I carry you back to your own fireside in the Land of Heroes?"

"If you will take me back to hear once more the silver-voiced cuckoos call, I will give you a helmet full of gold, or fill your cups with sparkling silver."

"Surely you are a wise and true Wizard, O Vainamoinen!" answered the old Witch craftily. "But I do not want your gold or silver. Can you forge for me the Sampo, with its many colored lid and its many many pictures, make it from the tips of the white swan's wing-plumes, from the magic milk of virtue, from a single grain of barley, from the finest wool of lambkins? If you can, I will give you my lovely daughter, the Rainbow Maiden, to go with you to the Land of Heroes, to hear the silver-voiced cuckoos sing."

"I cannot forge the Sampo with its lid of many colors," answered Vainamoinen. "But if you will take me back to my own home, I will send you the Wizard Blacksmith, Ilmarinen. He is a man of mighty muscle. None but he can wield the Heavy Hammer. He will forge the Sampo and beat its lid of many colors. He alone can win the lovely Rainbow Maiden!"

"I will give my darling daughter to him who can forge the Sampo," said the old Witch. "Go, send Ilmarinen here."

Then she harnessed a Magic Horse to her snow-white sledge of birch-wood, placed the ancient Vainamoinen on the sledge, and sent him homeward to the Land of Heroes.

And as he raced onward, onward, onward, rushing along the roadway, he heard the whizzing of a loom and the mocking of a voice. Lifting his eyes he saw a rainbow. On it was seated the Rainbow Maiden, lovelier than a dream, and dressed in a gold and silver air-gown. Merrily flew a golden shuttle to and fro in the Maiden's hands. She was weaving a web of finest, richest texture, with a weaving comb of silver. And she mocked the Great Wizard, as she rustled the silver webs of wondrous beauty, mocked him as he rode along, mocked him with many words of song and laughter.

"LISTEN now, O ye Lapp People!" cried the Red-Haired Wizard of Finland finishing this story. "Later I shall tell you another tale:

Tell you all of Ilmarinen,
Mighty Blacksmith, mighty forger,
Who could wield the Magic Hammer,
Weld the wondrous Magic Sampo,
Woo the mocking Rainbow Maiden.
Ilmarinen, strongest Wizard!

64

FORGING OF THE MAGIC SAMPO

CLING! CLING! CLING! CLANG! CLING!
Listen to the Red-Haired Wizard of the Land of a
Thousand Lakes!

In those first Golden Days, Vainamoinen, thinking bitterly on the Rainbow Maiden and her mocking, snapped his whip adorned with jewels, urged on his racing steed so that the snow-sledge creaked and rattled, and sped like lightning through fens and forests, over hills, through valleys, over marshes and mountains, over plains and meads, till at last he came to the Land of Heroes.

Then the Great Wizard began his Magic Incantations. He sang till a giant Fir Tree wondrous tall, grew up and pierced the clouds with its golden branches. Its shining limbs spread far and wide.

Then Vainamoinen sang again; sang the moon into the tree-top, sang the Great Bear's Stars entangled in its branches. Then he urged on his steed and hastened home to the heather-clad meadow in the Land of Heroes. He raced his steed up to Ilmarinen's smithy, and halted his sledge. He heard the breaking of coal, the roar of the bellows, and the blows of the Heavy Magic Hammer. The Great Wizard entered, and found Ilmarinen beating with his copper hammer on his forge.

"Welcome, Brother Wizard!" said Ilmarinen. "Why have you been gone so long? Where have you been hiding?"

"Many dreary days have I been wandering," answered Vainamoinen, "floating on the opal sea, and weeping in fens and woodlands. I have been visiting the Lapland folk, who are full of Magic. There I saw a lovely Maiden, who has refused the hand of many Heroes. All Lapland sings her praises. From her temples streams the moonlight, from her breast the sunshine, from her forehead shines a rainbow. On her neck sparkles a circlet of stars. Ilmarinen, go and see her! See her robes of silver and gold! See her seated on a bright rainbow and walking on purple clouds! If you will forge the Sampo for her, with its lid of many colors, you can win her and bring home a bride to your smithy."

"I know you, cunning, crafty Vainamoinen!" shouted Ilmarinen. "You have already promised me to the Lapland Witch to get yourself out of trouble! I will not go to see the Maiden. I will never go to dreary Lapland, where they eat one another."

"O, I can tell you of even a greater wonder!" said the crafty Vainamoinen. "I have seen a lofty wondrous Fir Tree with golden summit piercing the clouds. The moon and the Great Bear's stars are entangled in its branches."

"I won't believe your story," cried Ilmarinen, "unless I see the tree!"

"Come with me, and I will show it to you," said Vainamoinen.

Quickly they went to view the tree. Ilmarinen strode on before. He spied the glittering stars and gleaming moonlight entangled in its branches.

"Climb the tree, O Ilmarinen!" called Vainamoinen. "Bring down the golden moonshine and the Bear!"

And Ilmarinen straightway climbed and climbed and climbed the golden Fir Tree to the clouds.

Then quickly the Great Wizard began his Magic Incantations, sang a Magic Song of power, and summoned the Storm Wind to his help. He sang the Storm Wind blowing fiercely through the sky, sang:

Take, O Storm Wind, Ilmarinen!
In thy boat, O Wind, convey him,
In thy skiff, O Wind, remove him,

Quickly carry hence the Wizard,
To the very dreary Lapland,
To the gloomy Land of Witches.

And the Storm Wind darkened and made a boat of its clouds. It enfolded Ilmarinen, and sailed with him through the air to Lapland. Fast and furious travelled Ilmarinen in his cloud-boat, sweeping onward ever northward, till he alighted near the house of Louhi, the Old Witch.

Overjoyed she came out to meet him. She led him inside, and seated him at a well-filled table, that groaned with good things to eat. After she had fed him, she said:

"O Wizard Blacksmith, Ilmarinen, master of all forges and smithies! Can you forge the Magic Sampo with its lid of many colors and its many many pictures, from the tips of the white swan's wing-plumes, from the magic milk of virtue, from a single grain of barley, from the finest wool of lambkins? If so, I will give you my lovely daughter the Rainbow Maiden."

"Yes!" replied Ilmarinen. "I will forge the Magic Sampo with its lid of many colors and its many many pictures."

Then Ilmarinen, the mighty smith, hastened to set up his smithy on a large, colored rock. He built a fire and made a chimney. He laid his bellows and built a furnace.

Into the furnace he put the tips of a white swan's wing-plumes, the magic milk of virtue, a single grain of barley, and the finest wool of lambkins. Many wondrous forms, from day to day, these took within the furnace—first a golden crossbow with the brightness of moonbeams, then a purple skiff with copper oars, then a heifer with golden horns, then a beautiful plow, with handles of molten silver. But each was evil and did great mischief, till Ilmarinen broke them up and cast them back into the fire.

Then on the third day, Ilmarinen bending low, looked into the glowing furnace and saw the Magic Sampo rising with its lid of many colors.

Quickly with tongs he drew it from the fire, and beat and forged it on his anvil, beat it with his Magic Hammer.

So was forged the wondrous Magic Sampo. And it began to grind out treasures, wealth for the old Witch Louhi. From one side, it ground out fine flour; from its other side, flowed salt; from its third side, gushed glittering money.

Joyfully the old Witch grasped the Magic Sampo, and watched it grind and grind and grind. She took it far away and hid it in a copper-bearing mountain, and laid nine locks upon it.

Then Ilmarinen claimed his bride, the lovely Rainbow Maiden, saying:

"I have forged the Sampo. Will you come with me, my dear one?"

But she mocked him with songs and laughter, till he stood with bowed head, dejected, full of shame. And then the crafty old Witch, her Mother, put him in a copper boat. She sang the North Wind to her help. The North Wind came roaring furiously, and blew the copper boat to the Land of Heroes, to the smithy on the heather-clad meadow.

LISTEN to the Red-Haired Wizard of the Land of a Thousand Lakes! "Hear, O you Lapland people:

If you'd know how Ilmarinen
Gained the Rainbow Maiden scornful,
Set her on his Sledge of Magic,
Bore her off unto his smithy—
Read and sing the Kalevala;
Hero song of Finland's Wizards,
Magic Song from Land of Heroes!

If you'd know about the Sampo,
Magic Sampo, grinding ever,
Grinding treasures, grinding riches;

Know about the mighty battles,
Heroes' battles for the Sampo—
Read and sing the Kalevala,
Hero Song of Finland's Wizards,
Magic Song of Land of Heroes!

THE WIZARD WITH
THE LOLLING RED TONGUE

BOOM! BOOM! BOOM! BEAT! BEAT! BEAT! BOOM! BOOM!
BOOM!

So finished Kauko the Red-Haired Wizard of Finland, his Wonder
Stories.

And the Four Ancient Wizards of the South Baltic Lands, ground
their teeth, whistled, howled, and were still.

And while the Great Nischergurgje beat! beat! beat! on his Magic
Drum, and tapped! tapped! tapped! on his Magic Drum, the icy North
Wind rushed against the tent and blew the door-flap in. The Lapp folk
gathered closer around the fire. The flames flared up, and through the
smoke the people's faces showed strange and weird and their dark eyes
glowed.

Weeks had passed, while the Magic Stories were being told, and the
Lapp people did not know it!

Then Nischergurgje beat again with his golden drum-hammer, and
sang:

"I hear the rushing of the Storm Wings! Outside this tent, white
Winter reigns through the Long Dark Arctic Night. Deep snow lies on
mountain, vale, and marsh-land. Ice closes all streams. The Nail of the
North shines steadily over-head.

"Over the frozen, snowy deserts, the Lapp guides his raido of pack
reindeer—See! the string of reindeer, one deer behind the other, one deer

tied to the other. Across the hills and through the valleys, the laughing Lapp children on their skis, skim fast over the snow till the snow-lumps fly. The Lapp boys are hunting foxes. The hungry wolves snarl and chase the Lapp sledges. Boat-shaped, the sledges rock and sway as the swift reindeer gallop and their drivers snap the reins, while the Northern Lights flicker faintly and the full moon glides silently through the night sky. Always it is night, night, night!

"The Arctic cold strengthens. Gloominess descends upon us. Our hearts sink with heaviness. Clouds mass in the sky, and hide the stars and the flickering Lights. And while we wait for the golden sun to come back to us and lift our gloom, let us feast and tell tales."

And the feast was served again.

Then Nischergurgje, the tree-tall, tree-straight one, struck his golden hammer on his Drum, and cried out:

"Do you, Sarvik with back like an oak, woolly white hair, and lolling, red tongue, tell us Wonder Tales from your wonder land, the cliff-bound Estonia."

And the Four Ancient Wizards whistled, howled, ground their teeth, and were still.

And all the Lapp people were still and listened.

Sarvik hunched his back like an oak, wagled his woolly white head, and lolled his red tongue out.

Then he began.

WEIRD! WEIRD! WEIRD! EVER WEIRD!

FROM ESTONIA THE WISE AND THE FREE LAND OF ENCHANTMENT AND OF WONDER LEGENDS

Where the mystic cliffs are rising,
Where the billows beat and clammer,
Where they leap, and boil, and bubble,
In a Cavern, Crystal-Lighted,
Sings Estonia's Happy Wizard—
Sings a song of weird enchantments,
Sings of gnomes and magic serpents,
Sings of treasure and of mermaids,
Sings of fairies and of witches,
Sings of moons, and suns, and starlets,
Sings the mighty deeds of wonder
Wrought by strong and handsome Heroes,
In Estonia, Land of Magic,
In Estonia, Land of Wizards.

THE SINGING SWORD

WEIRD! WEIRD! WEIRD! EVER WEIRD!
Listen to Sarvik of the woolly white hair, and lolling red tongue!

In the ancient days of Wizards and Witches there lived, in Estonia, a giant Hero named Kalevide. His back was like an oak, his shoulders were gnarled and knotted, his arms like thick trees, his fingers spreading like branches, and his fingernails as tough as boxwood.

As for his huge Sword, he could whirl it around like a fiery wheel. It whistled through the air like a tempest. When he struck downward its keen edge was as lightning. A splendid sword worthy of the great Hero! It was wrought with the aid of powerful charms and tempered in seven different waters.

And for the Sword, he had paid a heroÕs price, four pairs of good pack horses, twenty milch kine, ten pairs of yoke oxen, and wheat, barley, rye, bracelets, gold coins, silver brooches, the third of a kingdom, and the dowries of three Maidens.

Now it once chanced that Kalevide with a load of heavy planks on his back, was travelling over the land. He reached the margin of Lake Peipis. Without waiting for a boat, he plunged into the water to his middle, and strode across to the other shore.

On the other shore an evil Wizard was hiding in the bushes. He saw the Giant Kalevide drawing nearer, looking huger and huger at each stride. The Wizard swelled his bristly body—bristly as a wild boar—stretched his wide mouth, and blinked his small upturned eyes, and muttered a Spell.

Instantly a Storm Wind swept over Lake Peipis. But Kalevide laughed a loud laugh at the wind, and said to the lake:

"You miserable little puddle, you are wetting belt!"

Then he stepped on land, and laid down his burden of planks, and trimmed off their edges with his Sword. After which he stretched himself out to rest.

The evil Wizard saw the gleam of the sharp Sword, and determined to steal it. So he slunk deeper into the forest to wait.

Kalevide refreshed himself with bread and milk from his wallet, loosened his belt, laid his Sword by his side, and soon fell asleep. Presently the ground shook with his snoring, the billows of the lake arose, and the forest echoed his snores.

Then the Wizard stole softly from the forest, and like a cat crept up to the sleeping Giant. He began to mutter Magic Spells and call the Sword to leave its master's side. But it would not move. Then he uttered stronger and stronger Spells. He scattered rowan-leaves, thyme, fern, and other Magic Herbs over the Sword. At last it moved and turned itself toward the Wizard. He grasped it in his arms.

But its great weight almost bore him to the ground. He struggled painfully along, step by step, dragging the Sword. By and by he reached a stream, and jumped over it. Splash! The Sword slipped from his arms and sank into the stream in its deepest place.

Then the Wizard began his Magic Spells again, and sang and muttered, and sang again. But the Sword would not return. Day dawned, and the Wizard fled into the forest.

When Kalevide awoke, he rubbed the sleep out of his eyes with his huge fists. He felt for his Sword. It was not there! He saw the marks where the Wizard had dragged the Sword along, so Kalevide rose up and followed them. And as he went along he called on his Sword to come back to its brother; he begged it to return, but there was no answer. Then he sang Magic Spells, but there was no reply. When he reached the stream, he saw the Sword gleaming at the bottom of the water.

Then Kalevide cried out to the Sword. asking who had stolen it and sunk it in the stream. And the Sword sang in reply that the Wizard had taken it, and that it had slipped from his grasp and fallen into the water,

"And now," sang the Sword, "I lie in the arms of the most beautiful of all Water Nymphs!"

"And does my Sword," sang Kalevide, "prefer the arms of a beautiful Water Nymph to the grasp of a Hero in battle?"

But the Sword refused to return, and Kalevide began his Incantations. He sang and sang, and he laid it on the Sword, that if any Heroes came to the stream, it must answer them; and if a singer came, it must sing; and if a Giant Hero came as great as Kalevide, it must rise up and be his Sword; but if the evil Wizard came, it must cut off both his legs.

Then Kalevide took up his load of planks, and went on his way. And where a waterfall came foaming over high rocks, the Three Sons of the Wizard met him. Two of them carried long whips with a big millstone fastened to each lash. There in deadly combat Kalevide overcame the Three Sons of the Wizard. Then he passed on.

Coming to a swamp, he felt tired, laid down his planks, and stretched himself out to sleep. And while he slept the evil Wizard crept to his side, and with Spells and Incantations threw him into a magic slumber.

And Kalevide dreamed of a better Sword than the first one, a Sword forged in the work shop of Ilmarinen, Finland's Wizard, forged in that wondrous workshop in the interior of a great mountain at the middle point of the earth. Seven strong smiths wrought it with seven copper hammers, and Ilmarinen, Finland's Wizard, watched every stroke of every hammer.

And so Kalevide dreamed on before he set out on other and greater adventures.

Many were his strange adventures;
Many Witches he outwitted;
Many Wizards fought and conquered;
Kalevide fair Estland's Hero!

THE MAIDEN OF THE MILKY WAY

THE stars shine down! The Northern Lights flash over the sky, and the Milky Way glows white! Listen to the song of the Wizard of the Crystal-Lighted Cavern!

Ah! Beautiful was Linda the lovely daughter of Uko. She showed all the skypaths to the little birds, when they came flocking home in the springtime or flew away in autumn. She cared as gently and tenderly for the little birds, as a mother cares for her children. And just as a flower bespangled with a thousand drops of dew shines and smiles in the morning sunshine, so Linda shone while caring for her little winged ones.

Thus it was no wonder that all the world loved Linda. Every youth wished her for his bride, and crowds of suitors came to woo her.

In a handsome coach with six brown horses, the Pole Star drove up, and brought ten gifts. But Linda sent him away, with hurried words:

"You always have to stay in the same place. You cannot move about," said she.

Then came the Moon in a silver coach drawn by ten brown horses. He brought her twenty gifts. But Linda refused the Moon, saying:

"You change your looks too often. You run in your same old way. You do not suit me.

Hardly had the Moon driven sorrowfully off, before the Sun drove up. In a golden coach with twenty red-gold horses, he rattled up to the door. He brought thirty presents with him. But all his pomp, shining splendor, and fine gifts did not help him. Linda said:

"I do not want you. You are like the Moon. Day after day you run in the same street."

So the Sun went away sorrowful.

Then at midnight, in a diamond coach drawn by a thousand white horses, came the Northern Lights. His coming was so magnificent, that Linda ran to the door to meet him. A whole coach-load of gold, silver, pearls and jewelled ornaments, the servants of the Northern Lights carried into the house and his gifts pleased her, and she let him woo her.

"You do not always travel in the same course," said Linda. "You flash where you will, and stop when you please. Each time you appear robed in new beauty and richness, and wear each time a different garment. And each time you ride about in a new coach with new horses. You are the true bridegroom!"

Then they celebrated their betrothal. But the Sun, Moon, and Pole Star looked sadly on. They envied the Northern Lights his happiness.

The Northern Lights could not stay long in the bride's house, for he had to hurry back to the sky. When he said farewell, he promised to return soon for the wedding, and to drive Linda back with him to his home in the North. Meanwhile, they were to prepare Linda's bridal garments.

Linda made her bridal robes, and waited and waited. One day followed the other, but the bridegroom did not come to hold the joyous wedding with his beloved. The winter passed, and the lovely spring adorned the earth with fresh beauty, while Linda waited in vain for her bridegroom. Nothing was seen of him!

Then she began to grieve bitterly and lament, and to sorrow day and night. She put on her bridal robes and white veil, and set the wreath on her head, and sat down in a meadow by a river. From her thousand tears little brooks ran into the valleys. In her deep heart-felt sorrow she thought only of her bridegroom.

The little birds flew tenderly about her head, brushing her with their soft wings, to comfort her. But she did not see them, nor did she take care of them any more. So the little birds wandered about, flying here, flying there, for they did not know what to do or where to go.

Uko, Linda's father, heard of her sorrow and how the little birds were untended. He ordered his Winds to fetch his daughter to him, to rescue her from such deep grief. And while Linda was sitting alone in the meadow weeping and lamenting, the Winds sank softly down beside her, and gently lifting her, bore her up and away. They laid her down in the blue sky.

And there is Linda now, dwelling in a sky-tent. Her white bridal veil spreads round her. And if you look up at the Milky Way, you will see Linda in her bridal robes. There she is, showing the way to little birds who wander.

Linda is happy! In winter she gazes towards the North. She waves her hand at the Northern Lights flashing nearer and nearer, then he again asks her to be his bride.

But though he flashes very close to Linda, heart to heart, he cannot carry her off. She must stay forever in the sky, robed in white, and must spread out her veil to make the Milky Way.

THE LUCK EGG

THE leaves of the Mystic Linden sigh! Light glows from the Magic Stone! Listen to the Wizard of the Crystal-Lighted Cavern!

Once on a time, in a great wood lived a poor man with his wife. God had given them eight children, and when a ninth was born, they were not overjoyed. But God had sent the child, so they had to receive him and give him Christian baptism. But there was no one willing to stand as godfather to such a poor child.

"I will take him to the Church anyway," thought the Father. "The Pastor may do as he chooses, christen him or not."

As he was starting out with the child, he met a beggar sitting by the way, who asked an alms of him.

"I have nothing to give you, little Brother," answered the poor man. "But if you will do me the favor of becoming my child's godfather, afterward we will go home and make merry with whatever my wife has provided for the christening feast."

The Beggar, who had never been asked before to be a godfather, was filled with joy, and went with him to the Church. Just as they reached it, what should drive up but a magnificent coach with four horses. Out of it stepped a young and noble Lady.

The man thought to himself, "Here, for the last time, I will try my luck!" Then he said to her humbly, "Noble Lady, will you take the trouble of standing godmother to my child?"

The Lady said, "Yes."

When the child was brought forward for baptism, every one was surprised to see a poor Beggar and a proud, noble Lady stand together as the child's godparents. The child received the name of Paertel. The rich Lady gave the child a christening gift of three gold pieces.

The Beggar went home with the poor man to enjoy the feast. And before he left that evening, he took from his pocket a little box wrapped in a rag. He gave the box to the child's Mother, saying:

"This is my christening gift. It is nothing much, but do not despise it, for it may bring your child great luck. A very wise Aunt of mine, who understood all kinds of Magic, gave me before her death the little egg in this box, saying:

"'When something unexpected happens, which you have never dreamed of, give this egg away. When it falls into the hands of him for whom it is meant, it will bring him great Good Luck. Guard the egg like the apple of your eye, and see that it does not break for its shell is tender.'

"Though I am nigh sixty years old," continued the Beggar, "never has anything unexpected happened to me till today, when I was asked to be godfather. My first thought was to give this egg to your child, as a christening gift."

The little Paertel throve, and grew up to be the joy of his parents. When he was ten years old, he was sent to a rich farmer to be herdboy. His Mother, when she was saying farewell, stuck the godfather's gift in his pocket, and bade him care for it like the apple of his eye. And Paertel did.

On the meadow where he grazed his herd, stood an ancient Linden Tree, and under this lay a great flint-stone. This spot, Paertel liked very much. The bread which he brought with him each morning, he ate on the stone, and he quenched his thirst at a little spring nearby. With the other herdboys, who were always up to mischief, Paertel had nothing to do. And it was wonderful that nowhere grew such beautiful grass as between the stone and the spring. Although his herd grazed there each day, on the next morning the grass had sprung up again green and fresh.

Now and then, when Paertel, on a hot day, napped a little, sitting on the stone, he was overjoyed by the most wonderful dreams. And when he woke, in his ears was the sound of music and singing, so that when he opened his eyes he seemed to dream on. The stone, too, seemed to him like a dear friend, which he said good-bye to each night with a heavy heart.

Paertel grew to be a fine lad, too old to be herdsboy any longer. The farmer took him as a farmhand. On Sundays and summer evenings when the other lads were joking with their sweethearts, Paertel did not join them but hurried off to his grazing meadow, to his beloved Linden Tree, under which he often spent half the night.

One Sunday evening as he sat on the stone playing upon his jew's-harp, a Milk White Snake crept from under the stone, raised its head as if listening, and gazed on Paertel with its clear eyes that glowed like fiery sparks.

Evening after evening, Paertel, as soon as he had free time, hurried to his stone, in order to see the beautiful White Snake. She became so used to him, that she would often wind herself about his leg.

By day he thought of the White Snake, and by night he dreamed of her. For this reason that winter seemed very long, while the deep snow lay on the frozen earth. As soon as the spring sunshine melted the snow and the ground thawed, Paertel hurried to the stone under the Linden Tree, although its leaves were not yet to be seen.

O joy! As soon as he breathed his longing through the harp the White Snake crept out from under the stone, and played about his feet. But it seemed to Paertel as if today the Snake shed tears, so his heart was sad.

After that he let no evening pass without going to the stone. The Snake grew so tame, that she let him stroke her. But when he tried to hold her, she slipped through his fingers and crept back under the stone.

On Midsummer Eve, all the village folk, old and young, went together to light the St. John's Fire. Paertel did not dare to remain behind, though his heart pulled him another way. But in the midst of the fun, while the others were singing, dancing, and having a jolly time, he slipped away to the Linden Tree, for that was the only spot where his heart found rest.

As he drew near it, he saw a clear bright fire gleaming from the stone. When he came closer, he saw the fire die down. It left neither ashes nor sparks. He sat down on the stone and began as usual to play on his harp. Instantly the fire blazed up again—it was but a burning from the eyes of the White Snake!

There the Snake was! She played his around his feet, and looked at him so beseechingly that she seemed to want to speak.

Midnight was near, when the Snake slipped under the stone and did not come back while Paertel played. Then he took his harp from his mouth, placed it in his pocket, and started to go home. Just then the leaves of the Linden Tree sighed so wonderfully in a puff of wind, that they sounded like a human voice. Paertel thought he heard them say over and over again:

Tender shell surrounds the Luck Egg.
Tough the heart of ancient trouble.
Take your Luck, while you may have it!

Then he felt such a painful longing that his heart seemed about to break. Yet he knew not what he longed for. Bitter tears ran down his cheeks, and he lamented:

"How can Luck help me, the Unlucky, for whom there is no Luck in this world?"

Then suddenly everything around him was as brilliant as if the Linden and the stone were the shining sun. For a minute his eyes were dazzled, then he saw standing near him on the stone, an exquisite maiden-shape in snow-white robes. From her mouth sounded a voice sweeter than the nightingale's. The voice said:

"Dear Lad! Do not fear, but listen to the prayer of an unhappy Maiden. Poor me! I live in a miserable prison. If you do not save me, I have no hope of escape. O dear Lad! Have pity on me, and do not refuse my request! I am the Daughter of a Mighty King of the East, who is immeasurably rich with gold and treasures. But those cannot help me, for I am bewitched in the shape of a Snake, and forced to live here under this stone. Here have I lived for many a hundred years, without growing old.

"Though I have never hurt a human being, every one who sees me flees from me. You are the only living mortal who has not fled. Yes! I have even dared to play about your feet, and your hand has stroked me! So there has arisen in my heart, the hope that you are to be my rescuer. Your heart is as pure as a child's, and in it is neither deceit nor falsehood. And the Luck Egg was your christening gift.

"Only once in twenty-five years," continued the sweet voice, "on the Night of St. John, am I permitted to assume my human shape, and to wander for one hour on earth. And should the lad with your gift come, and listen to my prayer, so might I be loosed from my prison. Save me! O save me!"

So speaking the maiden-shape fell at Paertel's feet, embraced his knees, and wept bitterly. Paertel's heart melted at the sight. He begged her to arise and tell him how he might rescue her.

"I would go through fire and water," cried he, "if that might save you! Had I ten lives to lose, I would give them all!"

The maiden-shape answered, "Come here tomorrow night at sundown. And when I creep toward you in the form of a Snake, and wind myself like a girdle around your body and kiss you three times, you must not be afraid nor shrink back. If you do, I shall again sigh under the curse of Enchantment for many a hundred years."

With these words, the maiden-shape vanished from the lad's eyes, and again the leaves of the Linden seemed to sigh and sigh:

Tender shell surrounds the Luck Egg.
Tough the heart of ancient trouble.
Take your Luck, while you may have it!

Paertel went home and lay down to sleep before dawn. But wonderful varied dreams, partly happy and partly horrible, chased sleep from his bed. He sprang up in terror when one dream showed him the white Snake winding its coils around his breast and smothering him.

However, he did not think more about this terrible thing, for he was firmly resolved to rescue the King's Daughter from the bonds of her Enchantment. Nevertheless, his heart grew heavier and heavier, the nearer the sun drew to the horizon.

At the set time he stood by the stone under the Linden Tree, and looking up toward Heaven, sighed and implored that he might not shiver or weaken when the Snake should wind herself around his body and kiss him. Then suddenly he thought of the Luck Egg. He drew the little box from his pocket, opened it, and took between his fingers the egg which was not larger than a sparrow's egg.

At that moment the Snow White Snake crept forth from under the stone, glided up and wound herself around his body. She raised her head to kiss him—when!—the lad himself did not know how it happened— he thrust the Luck Egg into her mouth.

He stood firm but with freezing heart, till the Snake had kissed him three times. Crash! Flash! Lightning seemed to strike the stone. Heavy thunder made the earth tremble. Paertel fell as if dead to the ground. He knew nothing of what happened around him.

But at this dreadful moment, the bond of Enchantment snapped, and the King's Daughter was freed from her prison.

When Paertel woke from his heavy swoon, he found himself lying on cushions of white silk in a magnificent glass room of a heavenly blue color. The beautiful King's Daughter was kneeling beside him and stroking his cheeks. As he opened his eyes, she cried out:

"Thanks! A thousand thanks, faithful lad, who freed me from my Enchantment! Take my whole Kingdom, take this Royal Palace and all its treasures! And take me, if you will for your bride! You shall live here happily, as is due the Lord of the Luck Egg."

Paertel's luck and joy had no end. The longings of his heart were stilled. Far from the world he dwelt with his dear bride in the Palace of Luck.

As for the people of his village, great was their astonishment when they went to search for him, and found neither Paertel, nor the Linden Tree, nor the stone. Even the little spring was gone. All had vanished away!

WOOD OF TONTLA

WEIRD! WEIRD! WEIRD! EVER WEIRD!
Listen now to the Wizard with the lolling red tongue!

WEIRD THINGS

In ancient days there was a beautiful wood called the Wood of Tontla. No one dared venture into it. The boldest men, who chanced to be near it, told how under the thick trees strange, human-shaped creatures swarmed like ants in an ant hill.

It happened one night that a peasant going home from a feast, wandered into the forest. He saw strange things! Around a bright fire countless swarms of children and old women were gathered. Some sat on the ground, others danced on the green sward. One old woman had a broad shovel in her hand, with which from time to time she scattered the glowing ashes over the grass. Then the children with a shout would mount into air and like night-owls flap about in the rising smoke. Then they would come back to earth again. Other strange sights he saw, but because the peasant's head was swimming, the village folk did not quite believe his tale.

Now not far from the Wood of Tontla, once lived a widower who had married a brawling, quarrelling woman. The seven-year-old little girl left by the first wife, was a bright, sweet creature. The wicked woman used to cuff and beat her from morning till night and give her worse food than she fed the dogs. As for the Father, he was too afraid of the wicked woman to help his child.

For two years Elsa stood this terrible life, and shed many tears.

It chanced one Sunday that she went with other village children to pick strawberries. Lagging along as children do, they reached the edge of the Wood of Tontla without knowing it. There grew many strawberries. The whole grass was quite red with them. The children ate the sweet berries, and filled their baskets with as many as they could. Then suddenly one of the boys recognized the dreadful place, and cried out:

"Run! Run! We are in the Tontla Wood!"

Those words were more terrible than thunder and lightning! All the children ran as though the Tontla monsters were at their heels.

Elsa, who had gone on a bit farther than the others, heard the cry of the boy, but she did not stop picking berries.

"The Tontla creatures," thought she, "cannot be worse than that hateful woman at home."

Just then a tiny black dog, with a silver bell hanging from his neck, came running up and barked at her.

At his barking a tiny Maiden in beautiful silken garments, sprang from among the trees, and told the dog to be quiet.

"How nice," said she to Elsa, "that you did not run away with the other children. Stay with me and be my playmate. We will play such pretty games, and go berry-picking every day. Mother will not refuse me this, when I ask her. Come, let us go to her now!"

Then the pretty child seized Elsa by the hand, and led her deeper and deeper into the wood. The tiny black dog barked for joy, and jumping on Elsa licked her hands.

O wonder of wonders! What marvels and magnificence met Elsa's eyes! She thought that she was in Heaven. A splendid Garden filled with fruit trees and berry bushes lay before her. On the boughs of the trees sat birds brighter than the most brilliant butterflies, many of them adorned with gold and silver. And the birds were quite tame, letting the children hold them in their hands.

In the midst of the Garden stood a Mansion built of rock crystal and precious stones, so that its walls and roof shone like the sun. A Lady in magnificent garments sat on a bench before the door.

"Whom do you bring as a guest?" she asked the little girl.

The little daughter answered, "I found her in the wood, and brought her here to be my playmate. Will you permit her to remain?"

The Lady smiled but said never a word. She examined Elsa with a sharp look from top to toe. Then she called Elsa nearer, and stroked her cheeks, and asked her kindly who she was, and if her parents were living, and whether she would like to stay.

Elsa kissed the Lady's hand and fell down before her, embraced her knees, and replied through her tears:

"My Mother has been resting for a long time beneath the grass.

Mother was carried away,
And all love went with her!

"My Father cannot help me, and the wicked woman at home beats me without mercy every day. So pray, golden Lady, let me stay here! Let me tend your flocks, or do any other work. I will do anything, and obey you. But do not send me home, or the wicked woman will beat me half to death, because I did not go back with the village children."

The Lady smiled and said, "I will think about it."

Then she arose and went into the house. The little girl said to Elsa:

"Mother is friendly. I saw by her looks that she will grant my request. Wait hear a minute."

And the little girl followed the Lady, then soon came back with a toy box in her hand.

"Have you ever been rowing on a sea?" she asked Elsa.

"Rowing on the sea! What is that?" said Elsa. "I have never heard of such a thing."

"O, you'll soon know!" said the little girl, and she took the cover off the box.

Inside lay a leaf of ladysmock, a mussel-shell, and two fishbones. On the leaf hung a few drops of water. The little girl spilled the drops on the grass. Immediately the Garden, the grass, and everything that stood there vanished. So far as the eye could reach, was only water, that stretched till it seemed to strike the horizon. Only under the children's feet was a tiny dry spot.

Now the little girl set the mussel-shell on the water, and took the fishbones in her hand. The mussel-shell swelled and changed into a pretty boat, big enough for a dozen children. The two children stepped into the boat. Elsa sat down timidly, but the little girl laughed, and the bones she held in her hand became oars. The waves rocked the children, like a cradle, and one by one little skiffs came sailing up. In each sat beings who sang and were joyful. Elsa could not understand what they said, but they kept repeating one word Kiisiki. Elsa asked what it meant and the little girl said:

"That is my name."

How long they rowed about I do not know, then they heard:

"Children, come home! It is nearly evening!"

Kiisiki took the little box from her pocket, in which the leaf lay. She dipped the leaf in the water till a few drops hung on it. Immediately they found themselves near the magnificent Mansion in the Garden. The water was gone, and all was firm and dry. The mussel-shell and the fishbones were back in box.

The children went into the Mansion.

THE MAGIC MAIDEN

IN a huge chamber sat four-and-twenty Ladies around a banquet table, all in splendid robes as though for a wedding. At the head of the table sat the Lady, Kiisiki's Mother, on a golden chair.

Elsa did not know what to look at first, everything around her was so magnificent and glittering. Upon the table stood thirteen dishes on gold and silver salvers. One dish alone remained untouched, and was carried away without its cover being lifted. Elsa ate all kinds of costly foods, which tasted better than sweet cakes. The four-and-twenty Ladies talked in low tones, and Elsa could not understand what they said.

Then the Lady, Kiisiki's Mother, spoke a few words to the maid who stood behind her chair. The maid hurried out and returned with a Little Old Man whose beard was longer than himself. He made a bow, and stood by the door. The Lady pointed a finger at Elsa, saying:

"Look carefully at this peasant child. I am going to adopt her. Make me an image of her, which tomorrow may be sent instead of her to her village."

The Old Man looked sharply at Elsa. Then he bowed and left the room.

After dinner, the kindly Lady said to Elsa, "Kiisiki has begged me to let her have you for a playmate. Is it really true that you wish to stay?"

Elsa fell on her knees, and kissed the Lady's feet and hands. But the Lady lifted her up, stroked her head and tear-stained cheeks, and said:

"If you will remain a good and diligent child, I shall care for you till you grow up. No misfortune shall touch you, and you shall learn with Kiisiki the finest handwork and other things."

Just then the Little Old Man came back carrying a trough of clay on his shoulder, and a little covered basket in his left hand. He set the clay and the basket on the floor, took a bit of the clay and shaped it into a doll. The Lady examined the doll on all sides, then said:

"Now we need one drop of the Maiden's own blood."

Elsa, when she heard these words, turned pale from fright. She was sure that she was about to sell her soul to the Evil One. But the Lady comforted her by saying:

"Fear nothing! We do not want your drop of blood for anything bad, only for your own future happiness."

Then she took a gold needle, stuck it into Elsa's arm, and gave it to the Little Old Man. He thrust the needle into the doll's heart. After that he laid the doll in the little basket to grow, and promised to show it to the Lady the next day.

Then they all went to rest. Elsa found herself on a soft bed in a sleeping-chamber.

The next morning, when she woke in the silk-covered bed with soft pillows, she opened her eyes and saw rich clothes lying on a chair nearby. At the same moment a maid stepped into the room, and bade her bathe herself and comb her hair. Then the maid clad her in the beautiful clothes. Her peasant clothes had been taken away during the night. What for? Now you shall hear!

Her own clothes had been put on the clay doll, which was to be sent to the village in her stead. During the night, the doll had grown bigger and bigger, till it was the very image of Elsa. It ran about like a human being. Elsa was frightened when she saw the doll so like herself, but the Lady noticing her terror, said:

"Fear nothing! This clay doll cannot hurt you. We are going to send it to your parents. The wicked woman may beat it all she wishes, for the clay doll can feel no pain."

So the clay image was sent to her parents.

GOLDEN WONDERS

From this day on Elsa lived as happily as the richest human child, that has been rocked in a golden cradle. She had neither sorrow nor care. Her former hard life seemed a dream.

But an unknown Magic Power appeared to govern the life around her. A huge granite stone stood near the Mansion. At every meal-time, the Little Old Man with a beard longer than himself, went up to the stone, drew a silver wand from his bosom, and struck the stone three times, so that it rang clearly. Then a great golden Cock sprang out and perched on the stone. Every time the Cock clapped his wings and crowed, something came out of the stone.

First a long table came all set with as many plates as there were people to eat. The table went of itself into the house, as if on the wings of the wind. When the Cock crowed a second time, chairs followed the table. After that platters of food following one another, all sprang out of the stone and flew like the wind to the table. Likewise flagons and apples and berries. Everything seemed alive, so that no one had to fetch or carry.

When all had eaten, the Little Old Man struck the stone again with his silver wand, and as the golden Cock crew, flagons, plates, platters, chairs, and table all returned and entered the stone, all except the thirteenth platter which had not been touched. A great black cat ran after that. The thirteenth platter and the cat sat down on the stone beside the Cock, till the Old Man took the platter in one hand, the cat under his arm, and the Cock on his shoulder. Then he vanished under the stone.

Elsa asked Kiisiki what all this meant, but Kiisiki said she did not know. It was a mystery.

The years flew by like swift arrows for Elsa in her happiness. She grew to be a blooming young girl. But Kiisiki stayed the same little child that she was when she found Elsa in the Tontla Wood.

One day the Lady sent for Elsa to her sleeping-chamber. Elsa marvelled at this, for she had never been sent for before. Her heart beat fast enough to burst. As she stepped over the threshold, she saw that the Lady's cheeks were flushed and tears stood in her eyes.

"Dear adopted Child!" said she. "The time has come for us to part."

"Part!" cried Elsa, throwing herself at the Lady's feet. "No! Beloved Lady, that can never be till death parts us. Why do you drive me away?"

"Child," said the Lady, "it is for your good. You are now grown up. You are a human being and can stay here no longer. You must go out among other human beings. You will find a beloved husband and live happily till the end of your days. We have human forms but we are not human beings."

Then the Lady combed Elsa's hair with a golden comb, and hung around her neck a small gold locket on a silken string, and she placed a seal ring on her finger. Then she called the Little Old Man, and pointed her finger at Elsa. She took leave of Elsa with sorrow.

Before Elsa could speak, the Little Old Man gently tapped her head three times with his silver wand. She felt herself changing into a bird. Out of her arms grew wings; her legs became eagle's legs with claws; her nose became a beak. Feathers clad her whole body. She rose suddenly in the air, soaring up towards the clouds like an eaglet just hatched from the egg.

So she flew southward for many days. She would have liked to rest when her wings grew tired. She felt no hunger. One day she was hovering over a low wood where hunting dogs were bellowing, when suddenly she felt an arrow pierce her feathers. She fell to earth. She fainted from terror.

When Elsa woke from her swoon and opened her eyes, she found herself in her own human form again, lying among bushes. How she came there seemed a dream. Then a handsome King's Son came riding up, and offered Elsa his hand, saying:

"It was a happy hour this morning when I started forth! Every night, I have dreamed of you, beautiful Maiden, for half a year; dreamed that I should find you here in this wood. Today I shot a great eagle which seemed to fall on this very spot. I hurried to get my booty, and found instead of the eagle—you!"

Then he placed Elsa on his horse, and rode with her to the city, where the old King welcomed her. A few days later the marriage was celebrated magnificently. On the wedding morning arrived fifty cart-loads of costly treasures, sent to Elsa by her adopted Mother.

After the old King's death, Elsa was Queen. But the Wood of Tontla was never seen nor heard of again.

WEIRD! WEIRD! WEIRD! EVER WEIRD! sang the Wizard of the Crystal-Lighted Cavern.

THE WIZARD WITH YELLOW EYEBALLS AND GREEN HAIR

BOOM! BOOM! BOOM! BEAT! BEAT! BEAT!
BOOM! BOOM! BOOM!

So finished Sarvik with back like an oak, and lolling red tongue, his Wonder Stories.

And the Four Ancient Wizards of the South Baltic Lands, ground their teeth, whistled, howled, and were still.

Beat! Beat! Beat! And as the Great Nischergurgje struck his Drum with his golden drum-hammer, a gray light fell through the smoke-hole in the top of the tent. The fire died down and its gray, gray smoke curled upward, out of the smoke hole, and mixed with the gray light.

And the Lapp people looked up, and cried:

"Ah-a-a-a-a-a-a-a-a-a-a-a-a-a-a-a!"

And their faces looked gray and weird in the strange light, and their eyes looked queer and gray through the smoke.

Weeks had passed while the Magic Stories were being told, and the Lapp people did not know it!

"Lo! the gray dawn comes!" shouted Nischergurgje as he struck his Magic Drum. "The Sun is not dead! He has turned his course. He is coming back. The Long Night, so sad and gloomy, will soon be ended. See! The pack reindeer are butting their horns into the birch thickets and the willow bushes; it bodes the coming of spring. See! The young fawns are lying on their sides, their legs as straight as arrows; it bodes the coming of flowers.

"Now, let the feast be served and tales told, while we wait for the golden sun to show his face above the rim of the world."

And the feast was served again.

Then Nischergurgje, the tree-tall, tree-straight one, called out:

"Kurbads, giant-strong, with yellow eyeballs and green hair, tell us Wonder Stories from your wonder land, Latvia of the crystal streams."

And the Four Ancient Wizards howled, whistled, ground their teeth, and were still.

And all the Lapp people said, "Ah-a-a-a-a-a!" and were still, and listened.

Kurbads, giant-strong, rolled his yellow eyeballs round and round, while each one of his green hairs stood on end and wriggled like a snake.

And he began:

GLEAM AND GLITTER! GLEAM AND
GLITTER! GLITTER! GLEAM!

FROM LATVIA OF FEAST OF FLOWERS AND COURLAND GOD'S OWN LITTLE COUNTRY

Kurbads, merry Lettland's Wizard,
With his Magic Incantations,
Calls the gold and silver to him;
Calls the jewels and the amber;
Calls the casks all filled with riches;
And they lie in heaps before him,
There they shine and gleam and glitter.

Then he summons all his Witches,
Old and wrinkled, toothless, grinning,
Bids them bide away the Treasures
In the ruins of the castles,
Underneath the ancient stone-heaps,
In the deep and dismal caverns.

Then he throws a Spell upon them,
Binds the Treasures with his Magic,
That no mortal eye may spy them,
And no mortal Song unloose them.
Thus he hoards his glittering wonders,
With his Magic Incantations,
Kurbads, merry Lettland's Wizard!

THE GOLD AXE

GLITTER! SHINE! SHINE! GLITTER!
Listen to the Wizard with yellow eyeballs and green hair!

Once on a time, in a farmhouse, a young Maiden sat spinning by the light of a burning pine-splinter. The farmer's wife and her daughter—the farmer had been dead for three years—were asleep already, for they were very lazy and liked to play the grand lady.

They always put off all the household tasks on the Maiden, who from sun-up to midnight had to keep her hands busy, without ever satisfying those who provided her with bread. If she did anything well and carefully, it was always, "What of it? Bestir yourself and finish the rest." And at the very least fault, it was scoldings and blows.

What was there to do? Ilsa, for that was the Maiden's name, had no parents and was poor. So she had to endure both the bad and the good. And there was a special reason why this was hard—the neighbor's son, a brave, handsome lad, would have her for his wife if his parents were not against it. It was not fitting, they thought, that the heir to a farm should woo a poor girl. He should bring home a farmer's daughter. And she was already chosen—no other than the daughter of the Maiden's Mistress. The wedding was to take place at Easter.

Ilsa loved the good Hans with all her heart, but she had to shut away her feelings in her breast, from the eyes and ears of the world. She was, yes! a poor orphan. Who cared to ask after her weal or woe? So Ilsa sat brooding at the spinning-wheel, while the icy North Wind howled and

103

raged around the house, and whirled the flocks of snowflakes against its walls.

Many bitter tears fell on the flax, many heavy sighs ascended to the low smoke-blackened rafters. Till from the sighs and tears there was formed a sad complaining little song:

See! The sun is hurrying on.
Let me to the shadows flee!
Little Mother can no more
In the sunshine lead poor me.

Wait! O wait, thou hurrying sun!
To my words, O listen! hear!
Take a thousand greetings sweet,
To my little Mother dear.

Low sets the sun—so very low!
Little Mother's far away.
I cannot overtake the sun,
Nor words to little Mother say!

The hoarse voice of the Mistress growled from her room, "To the Evil One with your sing-song!"

The daughter then began to scold, "If you will complain, go outside and howl with the North Wind."

Ilsa was silent and tried to spin on, but eyes and hands refused their service. Tired, she leaned her blond golden head against the hard wall, and closed her eyes. The pine-splinter had burned down and gone out, and it was dark in the room. Outside the North Wind howled and raged.

It was about six o'clock in the morning when the Maiden was startled out of her sleep, by a knocking on the little window. She stepped outside, but in the darkness of the winter morning could see no one. A trembling voice like an old beggar's fell on her ear:

"Pity me, dear Maiden, a lost, hungry, nigh-frozen, old man!"

Ilsa thought for a moment. She knew well that her Mistress never gave anything to a beggar, but chased any beggar from the house with insults and jeering. But she and her daughter were sleeping now, and would certainly not get up till seven o'clock.

"Come with me to the cow stable, Old Man," Ilsa said compassionately. "There you may warm yourself, and I will give you some bread and milk."

She let the benumbed old man into the stable, let him sit down on an overturned bucket, and milked some milk into a bowl. Then she fetched from the house a bit of bread, which the night before, in her great sorrow, she had not been able to choke down.

The beggar refreshed himself, and warmed himself as best he was able. Then he said to Ilsa, but not in a trembling voice, no! but with musical accents:

"Receive my thanks for your pity and your charity. I am not he for whom you take me. Who I am, however, it is not necessary for you to learn. But this I may say, I know you and all that your heart thinks and feels. I wish your happiness. Listen, now, to my words! Have you never heard of Lauskis and his Gold Axe?"

Ilsa said, "No."

"Lauskis is a Spirit of the Cold, who, when the frost is strong, goes about cracking the earth with his Gold Axe. If a young and innocent Maiden at midnight, just between the first and twelfth stroke of the hour, runs three times around the house, it comes about that Lauskis the Frost Spirit loses his Axe. This Axe is fashioned out of rich heavy gold, and whoever finds it will receive for it many thousands of gold pieces. Only innocence, courage, and swiftness can win it."

So spoke the old man.

Ilsa gazed on him in wonderment. But where was he? The bucket on which he had been sitting was empty! And the dull light of dawn showed no trace of him. The young girl involuntarily said a short prayer, and went back thoughtfully to the house. There was the mistress already up, and the every-day misery began again. So the winter passed away.

The stormy January was followed by a bitter cold February. At night the earth cracked and the ice burst on the pond. One day the Mistress and her daughter went to the city to buy a few trinkets for the wedding. They were not to return till the next afternoon. Ilsa was left all alone in the house.

That evening while she was spinning, the half-forgotten tale of the strange old man came back to her, and the longer she thought of his words, the greater grew in her an irresistible desire to run a race with the Lauskis.

The hours till midnight went by like a dream. Just as the old wall-clock in the Mistress' room struck, the Maiden rushed out and hurried like the wind three times around the house.

There came such a fearful crash! House, stable, and corncrib trembled and began to rock to and fro. Ilsa could scarcely keep herself upright by holding on to the doorposts.

But soon this was all over. The moon shone out sharp and clear, as it does only in the Northland winter, and it shone on a magnificent Gold Axe lying directly at Ilsa's feet.

At Easter-time the neighbors celebrated the wedding of Hans, not to the daughter of the farmer's wife, but to the long despised Maiden, the poor orphan, now the richest girl in the neighborhood.

As the years passed the pair lived happily and contented; and if they are not dead they are living today.

CASTLE-TREASURE

GLEAM! GLITTER! GLEAM! GLITTER! GLEAM!
Listen to the Treasure-Wizard:

It happened once on a time, that while a Lady was visiting late, her Coachman stretched himself out in the coach and went to sleep. Near midnight a voice waked him, saying:

"Get up! Come with me to Kokenhusen. I will give you money."

The Coachman sat up and saw that a Horseman had stopped his horse near the coach.

"Who knows," thought he, "what kind of a man this is, or what kind of money he offers me!" So he answered, "No, it is night time. I do not drive about with strange people at night."

The Horseman rode away.

The next night, at the same time, the Horseman woke the Coachman again.

"Get up! Come with me to the church yard. Money is there!"

"Well," thought the Coachman, "the churchyard is not far away. One can go there and back in half an hour."

"Good!" he said to the Horseman, "I will go."

He mounted his horse, and they both rode away.

Hardly were they out of town, before the strange Horseman gave his horse the rein, so that the sparks flew. The Coachman could hardly keep up with him. So they raced on and on, till they came to the churchyard.

Suddenly a bright light like day streamed around them. A whole host of people were coming towards them, crowd after crowd.

The Coachman was ashamed, for were not he and the Horseman riding fast like rogues?

"Let the cuckoo take the money!" he said to himself, and, turning his horse, galloped back as fast as he could.

Just as he reached the stable, the brightness and all the people disappeared, and it was dark night again.

But the Horseman would not let the Coachman rest. On the third night he appeared again, and waked him.

"Get up!" And as the Coachman opened his eyes, he added, "Good! Twice you have disobeyed me. Now listen to my counsel. When you come to Kokenhusen, go into the Castle at midnight. You will find cellar stairs. Descend. There you will see an iron door, on which hangs a bunch of keys. Open the door and go into the cellar. There you will find many cornbins full of gold and silver money. To be sure a Great Black Hound watches it. But do not be afraid, just step up and take all the money you wish." So spoke the Horseman, and vanished.

The Coachman thought, "That is a wonderful matter! Sometime I shall surely go into that Castle!"

It happened in a few days that the Lady went to Kokenhusen, and the Coachman drove her. About midnight, he went to the Castle. As he walked along the walls, he turned into the very cellar stairs. He descended. Yes! There was the iron door and the very bunch of keys!

He opened the door and stepped in. O wonders! O marvels! What treasure was heaped up there!

On one side of the cellar stood a cornbin full of money—full of gold and silver money that had been poured in like grain! But on the heap of money, lay a Great Black Hound watching. The Coachman drew nearer, but immediately the Hound raised his head and showed his teeth.

The Coachman stood thinking and thinking. How willing he would have been to take some of that money! But he was afraid to walk up to the cornbin and dip his hands into the heap of money.

So he turned round, left the cellar without taking anything with him, and went home.

The next day he visited the Castle again, and searched for the cellar. But he searched in vain. All he found was one old coin in a far corner of the Castle. The strange Horseman had left it there as a token!

WHAT WITCHES TELL

CLACK! CLACK! CLACK! CHATTER! CLACK!
Listen to the Lettland Witches!

In the Land where on Midsummer Night, the St. John's Fires blaze up, and the girls dance at the Flower Feast, adorned with garlands of wheat-ears and blue cornflowers, in that Land, I say, Witches fly about at the midnight hour.

There were once two brothers, who wished to go out into the world to try their luck. They thrust the blades of their knives into the trunk of a mighty fir tree, and made this compact: Whichever one of them should return first, he was to look at the blade of the other's knife. If bright, then his brother was alive.

They separated, and each went his own way.

The younger lad wandered through many strange lands, without gaining anything, and returned sadly to his home. When he reached the fir tree, he saw that the knife-blade of his brother was bright, so his brother was alive. Because darkness was drawing near, the lad decided to pass the night under the fir.

It was St. John's Night. After he had slept a few hours, about midnight, a rustling and a chattering woke him. He looked up and saw a flock of Magpies noisily settling on top of the fir. For a while he listened to their chatter, till it seemed to him that he could gradually understand what they said.

110

"Do you know any news, Sister?" said the first Magpie. "Not far from here, towards the west, stands a great and beautiful city. It has an abundance of everything. It lacks only water. This lack can easily be supplied. Upon the plain near the city, stands a huge Linden. If any one digs at its foot, a whole stream of water will gush up."

"Yes—yes—but have you heard my news?" said the second Magpie. "Not far from that city, to the east, is a high mountain, in which are treasures of all kinds. No one knows how to win his way into the mountain. And yet it is so easy! One needs only on the morning of St. George's Day, to plow three furrows round the mountain, and it will open. Then its treasures will belong to the plowman."

And so on, till each Magpie told her news! Then the birds grew restless, flapped their wings, and flew away. The lad under the tree perceived that they were no ordinary Magpies, but Witches who on St. John's Night fly about and tell each other the news.

Day began to dawn, and the lad was up and away to find the city described by the Witch. It was not long before he found himself in its beautiful streets. He stepped into a house and asked for a drink of water.

"You are certainly a stranger," was the answer given him, "if you do not know our need. We have an abundance of everything, only water is lacking. So we suffer a burning thirst!"

The lad then betook himself to the marketplace, and asked the people:

"What will you give me, if I produce water for you?"

The councilmen offered him a great reward, followed the lad to the huge Linden outside the city. At its foot, he had a deep pit dug. Instantly a powerful jet of water shot upward, and began to roar loudly. Then a stream of fresh clear water gushed toward the city and into it, destroying walls and houses.

Workmen soon checked the fury of the released water, and made a channel for it. The greatest joy reigned among the people, and the lad was given honors and money.

The lad remained for some time in the city, enjoying himself. But he still thought about what the second Witch had said. Taking a horse and plow, he set out to seek the mountain.

Soon he reached it, and on the morning of St. George's Day, he plowed three furrows round it. Immediately the mountain opened, and displayed a countless rich treasure—silver, gold, precious stones, in heaps and piles. Now was the poor lad become richer than the richest man on earth, and could lead a real, carefree life.

One day, when he was driving for pleasure along the highway in his magnificent coach drawn by six spans of horses, he met a poor wanderer leading along a colt. This wanderer was the elder brother, who had gained nothing in foreign parts except this colt. The rich one, when he recognized his brother, had the coach stopped, and asked:

"How do you come here? What has happened to you? What have you gained?"

The poor man looked sorrowfully at the colt, and said:

"This is all that I have gained in foreign parts."

Then the rich one related to him, that after he himself had wandered about for nearly a year as poor as a mouse, the Witched in the fir-top had told each other news. Things had gone well with him since then!

The elder brother listened carefully, and thought to himself, "If this one, who is younger and stupider than I, can win such Luck, why cannot I, who am wiser and older, win much more? I shall certainly get much more treasure than he did."

Then in shame and rage he slew the colt. After that he set out on his way. On St. John's Night, he came to the same fir tree, and lay own under it as if to sleep.

About midnight, as before, the flock of Magpies came flying up chattering and flapping their wings, and settled in the treetop. Then the birds began to talk.

"Do you know, Sister," said one, "what my news is this year? What we told a year ago about the water-poor city and the treasure-rich mountain, some one must have listened to. For a lad has given water to the city, and has taken its treasure from the mountain. We must be more careful. After this we must look under the trees. Perhaps there is a listener here now!"

And with frightful chattering, the whole flock of Magpies flew down to earth. There they found the elder brother.

That was the end of him!

LITTLE WHITE DOG

CHIME! CHIME! CHIME!
Listen to the Wizard of the Magic Incantations!

Once on a time there was a girl who lived with a bad-tempered woman. The woman treated her meanly. The girl tried to do everything she was told to do, but could never satisfy the woman.

One day she had to go to the well to fetch water without wetting the bucket. The poor girl shed hot tears. Just then a Little White Dog, as if called by magic, came running up out of the ground.

"If you will take me for your bridegroom,", said he, "I will provide water in your dry bucket."

The girl promised.

Then the Little Dog did as he promised, and vanished.

Some time after this, another bridegroom asked for the hand of the girl. She did not want him, but the wicked woman made her take him. There was nothing else to do!

The evening before the wedding, the bridegroom arrived. All hastened out to meet him. The Little White Dog appeared before the house. Every one went inside, but the Little White Dog was left without.

By and by the Little Dog began to sing:

Let me in, you pretty Maiden,
Me, your mannikin so wee!
Don't you know what at the fountain,
You so truly promised me?

Everybody laughed at the pertness of the Little Dog, and for a joke let him in. The Little Dog ran into the room, and saw the bridegroom sitting by the bride, and sang again:

Darling Maiden, seat me by you,
Me, your mannikin so wee!
Don't you know what at the fountain,
You so truly promised me?

The bridegroom said, "That's a funny little dog! He may sit near us because he begs so prettily."

The Little Dog laid himself down at the feet of the bride, and kept mouse-still.

The next morning the betrothal took place. Then the little dog sang again:

Maiden, take me for your bridegroom,
Me, your mannikin so wee!
Don't you know what at the fountain,
You so truly promised me?

The bridegroom looked surprised at this, but said nothing. After the betrothal was over, the breakfast was served and the Little Dog sang once more:

Seat me at your table, Maiden,
Me, your mannikin so wee!
Don't you know what at the fountain,
You so truly promised me?

The bride seated him at the table, and there was quiet. After breakfast they all, every one, got into the carriage to drive to the Church for the wedding. Then the Little Dog began to sing:

Maiden, take me in the carriage,
Me, your mannikin so wee!
Don't you know what at the fountain,
You so truly promised me?

The bridegroom let the girl take the Little Dog into the carriage, and they all drove off. When they reached the Church the priest began the service. Then the Little Dog sang in a loud loud voice:

Maiden, you with me must marry,
Me, your mannikin so wee!
Don't you know what at the fountain,
You so truly promised me?

The priest asked the bride, "What is it you have promised? Tell me everything before I can marry you."

Then the girl confessed everything from A to Z. The wicked woman stamped the ground in rage. But there was nothing to do! The priest would not marry the girl, nor could the wicked woman beat her. In anger and spite the woman ran from the Church, and the Little Dog ran after her. She would have seized him, but at that very minute there drove up a superb coach drawn by eight horses.

A footman descended from the box, and begged the Little Dog to step into the coach. The Little Dog got in, and changed into a magnificent Prince. The girl was married to him, and he took her with him to his Golden Castle.

The Prince raised the first bridegroom to be Lord High Counselor, because he had been so kind to the Little White Dog, had fed him, let him lie at the feet of the bride, and had taken him up into the carriage.

THE DUCKLING WITH
GOLDEN FEATHERS

GLEAM GOLD! GLITTER GOLD! GLEAM!
Listen to the Wizard of the gleaming cavern:

Once on a time two King's children, a brother and a sister, lived with a hateful woman. She ill-treated the two children, though she loved her own daughter who was both dirty and ugly.

One day the two children said to each other, "Let us go away."

So they went and went, till they reached a crossroad, and there they parted with many tears. The brother took with him a portrait of his sister to remember her by, and started on his way.

The girl went and went and came to a great Castle, the windows of which were as dull as rusty iron. She entered the Castle; there was not a single soul in it! She carried water in and washed the windows, and cleaned the rooms for they also were quite black.

She had scrubbed eleven rooms, and was about to scrub the twelfth but its door was fastened with a piece of linden-bark. She loosed the fastening and opened the door. And when she opened it, she saw three Black Women sitting on chairs, and three black torches burning before them.

The first Woman said, "Maiden, your Good Fate has led you hither."

The Second said, "You are indeed beautiful, but you will be more beautiful."

The Third said, "You have beautiful hair, but in future you will have golden hair."

And, when the girl stept back again into the eleventh room, she saw in the mirror that she had grown more beautiful and that she had golden hair.

After which she left the Castle and returned home. When she reached the house, the hateful woman was standing at the door. She saw how beautiful the girl had become, so she received her kindly, and sent her own daughter to try her fortune.

That one went and went and came to the very same Castle with the dim windows. She did not wash the windows at all, instead she sauntered through the rooms looking at everything. At last she found the twelfth door fastened with a piece of linden-bark, went in, and saw the three Black Women, before each of whom burned a torch.

The First said, "Maiden, your Bad Fate has led you hither."

The Second said, "You are certainly hideous, but you will be more hideous."

The Third said, "You have ugly, short hair, but in future pig's bristles will grow all over our head."

And so it was! When she looked in the mirror in the other room, she saw that her head was like a pig's head. And when she reached home, her mother did not want to let such a disgusting creature in. When at last she did let her in, she put her in a room under the floor, so that no one might see her. She gave her things to eat secretly. But the beautiful girl henceforth she treated kindly.

Meanwhile the brother had voyaged over the sea and reached a Castle. There he had taken service with a King. The King held him in high honor.

Now the brother was caring so carefully for his sister's portrait, that he had it on a table always before his eyes. Whenever he had free time, he sat before it. This the other servants noticed, and carried the news to the

King. Then the King bade the servants get hold of the portrait secretly, and bring it to him. But the young servant always kept his room locked.

Then one evening, the King had him called quickly, and the brother in his haste forgot to lock his room. The other servants had been waiting for that. They took the portrait and gave it to the King. Then he had the young servant called again, and asked him whose picture it was, whether it was that of his bride.

The young servant answered, "No! It is the picture of my sister."

Then the King commanded him to take a ship and fetch his sister, as he wished to marry her.

Good! The brother sailed away, took his sister some golden clothes, and told her that she must sail back with him, for she was to become a Queen. The sister prepared for the journey, but just as she was going aboard, the hateful woman pushed her own daughter on the ship, saying:

"What do I want you for? Cross the sea with these, so that I may never, during life, see you again!"

So they set sail. But when the ship was in midocean, the ugly daughter of the hateful woman pushed the King's bride overboard into the water, and put on the golden clothes. But the real bride was not drowned. She was changed into a Golden Duckling, and swam along behind the ship.

The King came down to the shore to receive his bride. But when he saw the girl with the pig's head, in his rage he cast the brother into prison. In three days, the head of the traitor must be cut off!

Now in the King's Castle was a kitchen-girl called Anna Panninja, but everybody called her Antscha. On the first evening came a Golden Duckling flying into the kitchen, and said:

"Antscha Panninja, how fares it with my brother, the young servant?"

Antscha answered, "He sits in the prison, and in three days his head will be cut off.

When the Duckling heard that, she flew away sorrowful.

On the next night, the kitchen-girl was all alone in the kitchen. Then the Duckling came flying in, and asked again:

"Antscha Panninja, how fares it with my brother, the young servant?"

Antscha answered as before, "He sits in the prison, and in three days his head will be cut off."

Then said the Duckling, "Someone could save him, if I might be a human being! In this you must help. Tomorrow evening I will come just once more. Then take a distaff and break it in two. Throw the pieces over your shoulder, catch me, and I shall win a human form."

On the third evening came the Duckling flying into the kitchen, and asked again:

"Antscha Panninia, how fares it with my brother, the young servant?"

Then the kitchen-girl broke the distaff in two, and threw the pieces over her shoulder, then caught the Golden Duckling. It changed at once into a beautiful Maiden with golden hair, who begged the kitchen-girl to go to the King, and get the key of the prison, so that she might visit her dear brother.

The kitchen-girl related everything to the King, and he hurried down to see the beautiful Maiden. As soon as he cast eyes on her, he recognized her by the portrait, and knew she was the right bride, only much more beautiful than her portrait.

Then the King went with her to the prison, and with tears begged the young servant to forgive him. In the future he would hold him as a brother, and he would hand over to him half the Kingdom! The brother forgave him, of course, but said he had a Kingdom of his own, for his father had just died.

After that the King married his beautiful bride, and lived happily. But the ugly daughter he ordered torn to pieces by horses.

THE WIZARD WITH BUSHY GOLDEN HEAD
AND APPLE-RED CHEEKS

BOOM! BOOM! BOOM! BEAT! BEAT! BEAT!
Boom! Boom! Boom!

So ended Kurbads giant-strong, from Latvia of the crystal streams, his Wonder Stories.

The Four Ancient Wizards of the South Baltic Lands, ground their teeth, whistled, howled, and were still.

And the Great Nischergurgje struck his Magic Drum with his golden drum-hammer—Boom! Boom! Boom!—Boom! Boom! Boom!

Then a golden glow shone through the smoke-hole in the top of the tent. A ray of sunshine like a golden spear glided downward and lighted the faces of the Lapp children. And the Lapp men and Lapp women screamed and cried with joy. The Lapp children shouted, and held out their brown hands to play with the sun's bright ray and to warm them. And the little dogs barked, and all the Lapp folk screamed and shouted again.

Weeks had passed while the Magic Stories were being told, and the Lapp people did not know it!

And the Great Nischergurgje swayed to and fro with joy, and struck his Drum, and sang and sang:

"How beautiful is Lapland, silvery silent Lapland! The Long Night is departing! A rosy glow bathes the snow fields. See! The sun's golden face smiles over the peaks of the mountains! See! The rich bright colors shimmer over the snowy plains! The mountain slopes glow purple, the high tops of the mountains are gilded, the lower ones are veiled violet mist. On every birch and aspen hang crystals of ice that glow like sparkling colored jewels.

"The sun, the sun has come! Each day he will linger longer, till he stays day and night. Beautiful, beautiful is Lapland, silent, silvery Lapland, when the sun shows his golden face over the rim of the world!

"Come now, while we wait for the Long Summer Day, let the feast be served and tales be told."

And the feast was served again.

And the Four Ancient Wizards whistled, howled, ground their teeth, and were still.

And the Lapp people laughed and shook with joy, and were still, and listened.

Then Nischergurgje struck his Magic Drum, and called out:

"Jakamas with the bushy golden head, pointed eyes, and apple-red cheeks, tell us Wonder Tales from your wonder land, Lithuania of the fragrant amber."

Jakamas bowed his bushy golden head, winked and laughed with his pointed eyes, and swelled out his apple-red cheeks, and began.

FROM LITHUANIA OF THE FRAGRANT AMBER COAST THE AMBER WIZARD

See! O see! the Amber Wizard,
Lithuania's Amber Wizard,
How he shakes his head all golden,
Puffs his cheeks as red as apples,
Steps into the foaming wavelets,
Dives into the Baltic billows;
Downward, downward to the forests,
Ancient pine trees 'neath the waters,
Pine trees shedding balsam amber,
Fragrant amber, light as feathers!

And the Amber Wizard loosens
Lumps of amber, beads of amber,
Casts them upwards through the waters,
Casts them on the sandy seashore;
For the little ones to gather,
As they run beside the wavelets.
Then they rub the balsam amber,
Yellow amber, nut-brown amber,
Amber like the drops of honey,
Crying, "See it glow with shining!"
Crying, "Feel it tingle gently!"

Crying, "Smell it, weird and spicy!"
And the Amber Wizard watches,
Shakes his head all bright and golden,
Puffs his checks as red as apples,
Smiles, and tosses high the amber!

LUCK, LUCK IN THE RED COAT!

CHEEP! CHEEP! CHEEP!
under the doorsill! Listen to the Wizard with red, red cheeks!

There was once a man who had two sons. He led a lovely orderly life. He brought up his sons well, and gave them good teaching. At last he died. After his death, his children took over the property. They lived together, and never quarrelled.

So they lived on for some time. Then the elder wished to marry. He took a poor wife, but she pleased him. Not long after this, the younger married. He took a rich wife. She brought as her dowry three hundred cattle and many other things. Now that the two brothers were married, each received his portion of the property. Then they separated and each lived by himself.

Everything went well with the younger. He became richer and richer. But with the elder, things went downhill. At last he was a very poor man indeed. He had no more bread. His rickety hut was almost tumbled down, and his farm he had to lease. There was left him but a small garden, and he had nothing to plow it with.

With his brother, things were going better and better. His grain throve, his meadows grew green and his cattle increased. Ten yokes of oxen plowed his field.

Then thought the elder to himself, "I will go to my brother. Ten yokes of oxen are plowing his field. Perhaps he will lend me one ox, with which I may plow my garden. He is such a good man, and has given me bread more than once, and has helped me in my need!"

He went therefore to him, and said:

"Listen, dear Brother! My last miserable nag is no more, and I have nothing with which tp plow my garden. Ten yokes of oxen are plowing your field. Won't you lend me just one?"

"Well, why shouldn't I? Go to the field and take what you want."

The elder went there and met a servant.

"Stop!" said he to him, "Your master has given me those oxen to plow my garden."

"I will not let you have them."

"Why not? Who are you, that you dare to disobey your master?"

"I am your brother's Luck."

"And where is my Luck?" asked he.

"Oh! He lies over yonder by the bushes, and has on a red coat."

"Just you wait!" thought the elder brother to himself. "That Luck of my brother's plows his fields for him, while you loaf round, and are bringing me to ruin!"

Then he cut himself a good alder stick, went over to his Luck, and struck the red coat again and again—whack! whack! whack!

"Oh-o-o-o-o!" said the Luck. "What do you want of me?"

"Why don't you help me, Monster?"

"If you want me to help you, sell your farm and become a merchant."

Very good!

The man went home and immediately sold his garden. Then he bought a horse and wagon, set his wife and children in the wagon, took a leather bag and put in it all sorts of things—needles and little bark-shoes. Then he closed his hut, and started off. But he had gone only a little way, when he heard something cheeping, chirping inside his hut.

He thought to himself, "I certainly left nothing behind. What can be cheeping? I'll go back and see."

He went, looked about, and could see nothing.

Then he spoke up, "Who is cheeping here?"

"It is we, your Need and Misery," answered something from a corner.

"Aha! Why do you cheep?" he gave back.

"We want to go with you, and you have shut us up in the hut and left us behind."

"Crawl into my bag!" said the man.

Then Need and Misery slipped quick! slick! into the bag.

"Just you wait!" thought the man to himself. "You have tormented me till this day. Now I will repay you."

He dug a hole under the doorsill, and threw into it Need and Misery, bag and all, and filled up the hole.

Then he went back to his wagon, climbed in, and drove on. He drove and drove. By evening he reached a city. He put up for the night in a wretched hut by the roadside. Then he went into the city and bought bread. In the market he saw fish, and bought a huge, beautiful pike. He carried it home to his wife for her to dress and cook.

As she was cutting it up, she found in its stomach a diamond of indescribable magnificence. It sparkled even in the dark. She could not look at it enough, and set it in the window. Then they all sat down to eat their supper.

Just then a nobleman came driving past with six horses. He saw something shining in the window of the hut. It was not fire or a candle. He ordered the driver to stop, stepped down from the coach, and entered the hut. He talked for a few minutes then asked:

"What kind of a thing is that, lighting the window so brightly?"

"Gracious Sir, that is a costly thing, but I do not know its value."

"Will you sell it?"

"Well! Why not? I am a very poor man.

"Good! I will give you a farm with eight farmhands. Do you agree to that?"

"Thanks, gracious Sir, I do."

Then the nobleman bade him, his wife, and children take their seats in the coach, and he drove them to the farm he had promised.

There the man lived for a few years, as he was contented to do, and things went quite well with him. But he began to think that he must be a merchant. He sold the farm, drove to the city, opened a shop, and started to trade. He had such wonderful Luck that everything he bought for one ruble, he sold for two; and what he bought for twenty, he sold for forty.

So he lived on for some time, and became the very richest merchant in the city. The other merchants could do nothing without him, so they made him Chief of the Merchants.

About this time, the youngest brother came to the city with thirty loads of flax. The merhants were going to buy the flax, when they found much bad stuff mixed with it, and threw the poor man into prison. After three days they led him before the Chief of the Merchants, to pronounce judgment on him. The Chief recognized his own brother and thought of the good he had done. So he set him free, bought all his flax, and paid him well.

Then he took him home, entertained him, and gave him presents besides. When the younger brother was about to leave, he asked his elder brother:

"How have you come by such riches?"

The elder told him all that had happened.

When the younger brother reached home, he said to his wife:

"Listen! We live finely, but we cannot compare with my brother in anything. He deals in thousands. He is Chief of all the merchants. Besides he is a good man. God give him health! He freed me from my misfortune, entertained me richly, and bestowed presents on me."

"How could he become rich so quickly?" asked his wife.

"It came about in this way, he answered. "He has buried all his Need and Misery under the doorsill of his hut, and that has brought him Good Luck in everything."

This displeased his wife. Envy took hold of her.

"So-o! The brother had buried his Need and Misery had he? Well! She would let them out so they might go back to him. She hurried to the hut, dug, opened the bag, and said:

"Now Need and Misery, go back to the brother of my husband!"

"We cannot find him again," replied Need and Misery. "We would rather stay with you!"

And there they stayed! They drove the younger brother to poverty.

But the elder brother lived on with Good Luck, and was a merchant, and is one today.

POOR MAN AND NEVER-ENOUGH

SPLASH, SPLASH! SPLISH, SPLASH! SPLISH, SPLASH, SPLISH!
Listen to the Wizard with the apple-red cheeks!

Once on a time, a poor man went into the woods to the riverbank. He chopped down a tree, chop! chop! As he chopped, crick! crack! the axehead fell from its handle, splash! into the deep water of the river.

The poor man cried out, "Oh-o-o-o-o! My axe! A-a-a-a-a-a! Who will fish it out for me? My poor little axe!"

Just then, limpity, limpity! limp! a very very old man came limping up, and asked:

"Why do you yell so loud? What has happened to you?"

"Oh-o-o-o-o! My axehead is gone. It has fallen into the water, and I have nothing to buy another with. I am so poor! How can I chop down trees now, and earn bread for my children?"

"Be quiet! Stop yelling! I will fish it out for you."

And then—rip! rip! rip! the old man tore off his coat, and sprang, splish, splash! into the water. After a while, hippity, hop! he stood up in the water, and held Out a golden axehead.

"There! Take it! Isn't that your axe?"

"O no! O no! It isn't mine," answered the poor man.

Again, splish, splash! the old man dived under the water. After a while, hippity, hop! he stood up with an axehead of silver.

"It isn't mine!" cried the poor man hardly looking at it at all.

130

The third time, splish, splash! into the water, and the old man brought up the iron axehead.

"That is my little axe! That is my little axe!" shrieked the poor man full of joy. "Thanks be to you, that I have it again!"

He grasped the axe, snitch, snatch! from the old man's hand. Then right about face! Forward march! He started for his home. But:-

"Hi, there!" cried the old man after him. "Because you are such an honest, contented man, here, I'll give you these golden and silver axeheads."

When the poor man reached home, chit! chat! chit! how he chattered about it all! And a neighbor heard him, a greedy man, a Never-Enough.

The Never-Enough thought a bit, ran! rin! ran into the woods, and Aha! chopped a tree, chip! chop! in the same place. His axehead, which he had loosened, fell splash! into the water.

Then he began to yell, "Oh-o-o-o-o-o-o-o!"

Limpity, limpity! limp! the old man stood there.

"What has happened to you?"

"My own little axehead, splash! has fallen into the water and sunk. Who will find it for me?"

"I will!" cried the old man, and sprang splish, splash! into the water.

After a while, hippity, hop! there he was again in the water, with the iron axehead.

"Here is your axe."

"That isn't mine! That isn't mine! answered the Never-Enough.

Again, splish, splash! the old man in the water, and hippity, hop! after a while back again with the silver axehead!

"Is that yours?"

"It's not mine! Mine was different."

The third time, splish, splash, splish! the old man in the water, and hippity, hop! out of the water again with the golden axehead!

"That is mine!" cried the greey Never-Enough, full of joy.

And because he lied so shamelessly, hi there! the old man dived into the water, and did not come back.

As for the golden axehead, zip! it passed close to the nose of the Never-Enough. He kept on waiting, waiting, for some one to bring him a diamond axehead!

And maybe he is waiting there still!

LITTLE WHITE HORSE

GALLOP-A-TROT! GALLOP-A-TROT!
Listen to the merry, merry Wizard with the pointed eyes!

There was once a man who had three sons, two were clever, but the youngest was simple. The Father bought each of them two horses.

One day they heard that something was eating up their barley. The first night, the Father sent the eldest son to the field to watch the barley. But he fell asleep and saw nothing.

And the next day, when he came home and his Father asked, "Now what have you seen?" he said, "Nothing."

The second night, it was the second son who must watch, and he also saw nothing.

Now came the turn of the Simpleton. The Simpleton took a halter, went to the barley field, and sat down on a stone. There he sat till midnight. Just at midnight a White Horse came flying, and he was so white that the whole earth glowed with brightness. The Simpleton caught the White Horse.

Then the White Horse spoke:

"Set me free, and whenever you are in need I will help you. You have only to call, 'Little White Horse!' and at once I will be with you."

Then the Simpleton let the White Horse run away. And when, the next morning his Father asked him, "How now, Stupid, have you caught anything?" he answered:

"Yes, I have caught a White Horse. But he begged me so hard to let him go, that I set him loose."

One day the news came that the King would give his daughter in marriage to any lad who on horseback could leap from the castle courtyard to the third story. The Father let his two elder sons start out, Simpleton must stay at home. But he begged so hard that he might go along, that at last his Father consented.

After they started, Simpleton went off by himself, and called:

"Little White Horse!"

The Little White Horse came running. Simpleton crept into one of his ears and out at the other. And there he was, a handsome stately youth!

Then he rode to the King. Once in the courtyard, he gave the Little White Horse the spur in the flank, and sprang with him into the air, and leaped up to the third story to the King's Daughter. The King's Daughter gave him her ring, and he rode away home.

When he was not far from the house he left his horse. The lad now looked just as he always did.

Then he went into the kitchen and sat down by the stove where it was nice and warm, and started to examine the ring. He had wrapped up his finger on which was the ring, and now, when he unwrapped it, a bright light filled the whole kitchen. He covered the finger again, but his two brothers called out:

"Simpleton, what are you doing? You will certainly set the house on fire!"

One day after that, the King sent an invitation to a feast. The Father let his sons go, Simpleton too, and went along himself. Every one sat down to the table, except Simpleton who seated-himself by the stove.

Then the King's Daughter passed the cups to the guests, and when she came to Simpleton, she said to him:

"Why is your finger bound up?"

134

She unbound his finger, and there streamed forth a bright light over all those sitting in the room. When the King's Daughter saw that, she took Simpleton by the hand and led him to her Father, saying:

"This is my bridegroom."

After that she led him out of the room, washed him, put on him the most beautiful clothes, led him back into the room, and made him sit down at the table beside her.

And the Simpleton and the King's Daughter were married.

ONE HUNDRED HARES

HA! HA! HA! HA! HA! HA!
Listen to the laughing Wizard with the pointed eyes!

In old times there lived a King. He had only one daughter. He would not give her in marriage except to the man who could perform three great tasks even if he were most miserable of beggars. Many tried, but none succeeded.

Now not far away dwelt a poor man who had three sons. The eldest and wisest said:

"I am going to win the Princess."

On the way thither he met an old Beggar, and he never even said good morning to him.

The Beggar said, "Whither do you speed, my Son?"

"What business is that of yours?" he growled in passing.

The old one answered, "Your going will be in vain."

And so it was. The eldest and wisest returned home without having accomplished anything.

The second and wise son, now said he was going, and surely he would win the Princess. But it happened to him, as it had happened to the first.

Then the third and stupid son spoke:

"Since the two elder have been, I am going. Perhaps I shall succeed."

"What can you do, when the wisest could not succeed?"

But he did not ask for anything, and set out for the King. He met the old Beggar, bowed to him, took off his cap, and wished him a good morning.

The old man thanked him, and asked where he was going. The lad showed him his whole heart, he hid nothing. The Beggar then gave him a whistle, and said:

"Today you will have to tend a hundred hares. Just whistle to them, and they will obey you."

It happened as he said.

When the lad came to the King, the lad's first word was:

"Where is your daughter? I want to see her, whether she pleases me.

When he had looked at her he said, "She pleases me. For her sake I will perform the three tasks."

The King set him the task for that day, of tending a hundred hares. When they carried them to the field and turned them loose, the hares ran away in every direction.

At first the stupid son let them do as they wished; but when they were all out of sight, he wanted to see if they would obey him. He blew on his whistle, and the hares were there like lightning. He counted them, and missed none.

"Good! Run away again and feed. When I need you, I will whistle," said he to the hundred.

I do not know who saw all this and reported it to the King. But he was in a great rage. He sent his wife to the lad that she might ask and beg for a hare. She dressed herself like an old woman, came slyly to the lad, and asked if he would give her just one hare, she needed it so much!

He answered, "I can neither sell it nor give it. The hares are not mine."

She kept on begging and begging, "You could easily give me just one."

He marked who she was, and finally said he would give her a hare, if she would give him a hearty kiss. She said no! and no! but when she saw it was the only way out she gave him a kiss.

She stuffed the hare into a covered basket, and went away happy, thinking she had deceived the stupid lad. He waited till she was near home, drew out his whistle, and whistled hard. Bang! the hare sprang against the cover and, heigh ho! leaped back to his master. The Queen stood still with her mouth open. The hare was gone!

That evening the stupid lad chased his hundred hares home, and handed them over to the King.

The next morning the old Beggar came again. He gave the lad a horn to call together horses. That day the King set him the task of herding a hundred horses, and of driving them all home at evening.

When they let the horses loose in the field, they ran away in every direction. But in a little while the lad sounded his horn, and they all came galloping up and stood around him.

Then the King told his wife to go and beg for a horse. But she would not go. She said she was afraid of horses, that he should go. The King disguised himself so that no one should know him, and rode to the field where the lad was, and asked him if he had a horse to sell.

"I have none, for sale," said he.

Well, could it be borrowed?

No indeed!

Well, could it be given away?

"O if need be, I could give one, but only if you will kiss your donkey."

The King twisted his mouth this way and that. But it was of no use! He had to kiss the donkey, or he would get no horse.

When he had done this, he placed himself joyfully on the horse, rode home, and shut the animal in the stable, thinking:

"I have certainly deceived that lad! There will be one of his horses missing tonight!"

138

The youngest son, not knowing that the King had already reached home, sounded his horn soon after the horse was in the stable. When the horse heard the horn, he sprang against the door. The door opened crick, crack! and the King hearing the noise ran to the window. All he could see was the whisk of a tail.

In the evening the lad chased the horses home, and drove them together into the stable.

On the third day, the King ordered him to tell lies into an empty sack till he, the king, called out:

"Bind it!"

The lad stuck his mouth into the sack, lied and fibbed as hard as he could, but the sack stayed empty. Then it came into his head to fill the sack with truth!

He began to relate how he had tended hares, and how the Queen had come to buy, but that he had given her nothing till she kissed him!

Ha! ha! ha! The King roared with laughter, and enjoyed the shame of his wife.

Now the lad began to tell further, that while he was herding the horses the King himself had come to get a horse, but that he, the lad, had given him nothing till he—the donkey—

"Bind the sack, quick!" cried out the King before the lad could finish. "It is full!"

And so the lad won the Princess, as easily as rolling off a log.

MANNIKIN LONG BEARD

CRACK, BANG! SLAM, BANG! BANG, CRACK!
Listen to the laughing Wizard again!

In a certain village there was once a Land owner who had a wife. Though married long years, they had no child. Both of them grieved very much over this.

At last, however, the wife had a little son, whom she named Martin. The mother loved the child very much. He grew up to be so strong that no one could overcome him. When he was twenty years old, he felt a great longing to journey through the world, and begged his Father to have a smith make him a strong iron staff. Except for that, he did not want anything.

Then the father drove to town, bought some iron bars and gave them to the smith to make a staff. When it was ready, the strongest man could scarcely lift it. Martin, however, grasped the staff and swung it like a feather to and fro; then, to try it, threw it into the air. As it fell down he caught it, and broke it in two.

Now the Father must go to town to buy iron again and have it forged into a staff. This time it was just such a staff as Martin wanted. When it was ready, Martin, to test its strength, threw it into the air. Falling down, it struck so deep into the earth, that it was a day's work to dig it out.

Then Martin took leave of everybody, and set out on his travels.

After he had been on the road many days, he met a Smith who carried a huge hammer, and said that he was very strong. Then Martin proposed that they should travel along together. The Smith agreed to the proposal. As they went on together, Martin asked the Smith, how strong he really was.

The Smith said, "When with this hammer I give just three strokes to the biggest tree, that tree has got to fall!"

Martin said, "When you have chopped it, I'll stop it from falling with my great staff."

So it was in truth! When they came to a very great and thick tree, the Smith chopped it with three strokes, but Martin, as it fell propped it with his staff, so that it could not touch the ground. By this, both knew that both were strong.

As they wandered on farther together, they met a Tailor, who said that he was not very strong, but he could sew so swiftly that in one day he was able to dress a man from head to foot. That pleased Martin and the Smith, and they said:

"Come with us! We are both strong enough, and will let no misfortune harm you."

Then he went with them, and the three wandered far and wide. After a long time, they found in a wood a very neat little house. Its owners were dead. There was food aplenty on hand. They agreed to stay there as long as it pleased them. After they had been there a few days, it came into their heads to go hunting, to shoot game. One of them, of course, must stay at home and look after the food. They agreed that the one who knew the most about cooking should stay at home. The Tailor said:

"I understand that matter best, I am used to being in the kitchen with the housewives, and know well how to handle pots and pans."

"Good!" said the others. "Here you stay then, and boil and bake so that things will be tasty.

The next day, after breakfast, the Smith and Martin each took a gun and went to hunt in the wood. But the Tailor, at home, set about preparing the midday meal, and ran around with his apron tied in front just like a cook. He peeped into every corner, till he had brought together what he

141

neededd for the noon meal. He wished to take great pains and to cook everything tasty, so that the others should praise him.

When the pot stood over the fire and began to bubble, tap! tap! tap! some one knocked on the house door. But the Tailor could not leave the pot to see who it was, and thought:

"If it is a man, he can walk in for the door is open."

But as the knocking kept on, tap! tap! tap! after a while he stepped out. And see! Outside, before the doorsill, stood a foot-high Mannikin with a fathom-long beard. The Mannikin began to beg the Tailor to let him in the kitchen—he was so tired, so cold that he was perishing! And he seemed so miserable and weak, that he could not step over the doorsill. The Tailor had to carry him in.

Once in the kitchen, he moaned again sadly, and begged the Tailor to lift him on to the little bench, so that he might warm himself at the fire. The Tailor thought him such a poor, miserable thing that he lifted him very carefully on to the bench. When the Mannikin had warmed himself a little, he began to wail again—O! he was hungry!—and beg for a little bit of meat—then he would be all well again!

The Tailor took a piece that was a little done out of the pot, and gave him some of it with the words:

"There take that little bit. When the meat is done, you shall have all you want."

But Mannikin Long Beard trembled so, that the bit of meat fell out of his hand onto the floor. Then he begged the Tailor to pick the piece up.

The Tailor did so, but just as he bent over to pick up the meat— spang!—the Mannikin jumped from the bench onto the back of his neck, then began—ha! ha!—to pound him and pummel him with his fists. The Tailor screeched and scolded, but it was of no use.

The Mannikin struck and tormented him, till he fell to the floor half dead. And after Mannikin Long Beard had thus tortured and plagued his benefactor, he went away. No one knew where he went, or from whence he came!

When the Tailor had recovered a little, he crept on all fours to bed, and was sick.

Sometime after midday, the others came back from the hunt, and found their comrade very sick and whimpering. The fire on the hearth was out, the meat half cooked, and the soup good for nothing. Then both the hunters had a very poor midday meal, and they could not have eaten it at all, if they had not been so hungry. The Tailor, however, said nothing.

The next day, it was the Smith who had to stay at home and cook, while Martin and the Tailor went to hunt.

While the Smith was cooking, tap! tap! tap! some one knocked again on the housedoor. The Smith had no time to see who it was. But as the knocking kept up, he went out to find who was there. And see! The Mannikin was there again. But the Smith did not know anything about him!

Mannikin Long Beard pretended again, as he had done the day before, and the Smith was as full of pity for him as the Tailor had been. The Smith lifted him on to the bench, gave him a little piece of meat. And when the Mannikin let it fall on purpose, as though he could not hold it in his trembling hand, the Smith bent down to pick it up—and then!

Spang!—Mannikin Long Beard leaped on the back of his neck. The Smith tried in every way to tear him off his back, but it was of no use! Mannikin Long Beard struck, squeezed, pinched, and tortured him, till all strength left the Smith and he tumbled down nearly dead. Mannikin Long Beard stopped.

The Smith was so badly hurt, that for a long time he lay on the floor. Then he came to himself enough to crawl on all fours to bed.

When the two others came home, they found him lying in bed, and nothing ready. For right in the middle of the cooking had the misfortune befallen the Smith. But though the Smith said iiothin, the Tailor knew right well what had happened. And to the Smith, it was clear why the Tailor had been sick the day before.

When Martin found the Smith in such a bad state, he cared for him, and by evening he was much better.

On the third day, it was Martin who had to stay at home and do the cooking. And just when the food was set over the fire and had begun to cook, came Mannikin Long Beard to the house and knocked—tap! tap! tap!

Martin, however, took his time, and let him knock a very long while. Then when Martin was tired of hearing the knock! knock! knock! he went out to see who was there. And he was not surprised to find Mannikin Long Beard before the doorsill. He spoke roughly to him:

"What kind of a thing are you? Where do you come from? Now I see well, who hurt my comrades yesterday and the day before."

When Mannikin Long Beard heard that, he began to tremble all over his body, so that his very long beard waggled. He howled and moaned so a stone would have had pity, saying:

"I know nothing about it! I am forsaken of all the world, despised and laughed at. I don't dare to show myself among people. I have come here quite by chance, and have lost my way. Oh, pity me! Let me in the kitchen so I can warm myself a bit! Yes! I am so cold-so very cold!"

When Martin saw him trembling, and howling, and heard his bitter pleading, he thought:

"The creature is really miserable!" So full of pity he said to him, "There! there! come into the kitchen."

But Mannikin Long Beard said, "Oh! I am tired, and so weak, that I cannot step over the doorsill! Be good enough to carry me in."

"That is it, is it, you howling creature? Come in if you want to; and if you don't, why, stay where you are!"

As Martin said that, he went into the kitchen, poked the fire under the pot, the fire had nearly gone out, and began to skim the scum off the soup. Then Mannikin Long Beard, standing before the house, began to

144

wail sadly, and to howl, and to plead that Martin would lift him up on the bench by the chimney, so that he might warm himself by the fire.

Martin seized him by the beard, and lifted him onto the bench. Then he warmed himself by the fire, and began to flatter Martin, to speak friendly to him, and kiss his hands. But Martin was suspicious of all this. And when Mannikin Long Beard talked too much and crept into the chimney, he seized him by the beard, lifted him in the air, and set him down down hard on the bench, saying:

"If you crawl into the chimney again, I will fling you like dirt out of the window."

For a little while there was peace. Then Mannikin Long Beard began to beg Martin for just one little bite of meat—if he did not have it, then he should die of hunger! Martin threatened him with the skimmer in his hand, and said:

"Do you see this ladle? Wait till the meat is done, then you shall have some."

But Mannikin Long Beard kept on whimpering—indeed Martin might give him just a bite of bread, he was so faint! Martin took, meanwhile, a piece of meat from the pot, tried it to see if it was tender, cut off a bit and put it in the Mannikin's hand.

Then the Mannikin, on purpose, let the meat fall out of his hand to the floor, making his hands tremble as if still benumbed by the cold.

Martin was very angry and said, "Come now, you good-for-nothing! Am I your servant?"

He stamped with his boot on the floor hard enough almost to overthrow the stove, grasped the Mannikin's beard, and shook him.

Then Martin stooped to pick up the piece of meat from the floor, but without taking his eye off Mannikin Long Beard. Spang!—The Mannikin would have leaped on his neck, but before he could land on his back, Martin caught him by the beard.

Then there was the biggest tussle you ever saw! Twist! Turn! Wrestle! Martin had to use his great strength to reach for his staff. Then—whack!

crack! bang!—he gave the Mannikin the worst drubbing! He beat him till at last the Mannikin had to beg Martin to stop.

Martin took up an axe in his right hand, held Mannikin Long Beard in the left, carried him out, and—whack! bang! whack!—he chopped a cleft in a big tree-stump. In the cleft, he squeezed Mannikin Long Beard's beard, and left him there hanging to the stump.

After this work, Martin prepared the midday meal, then sat down to rest, for the struggle with Mannikin Long Beard had tired him. Yet he rejoiced that he had overcome him, and that now he would be able to show the little monster to the others.

Meanwhile the Smith and the Tailor had told each other about Mannikin Long Beard, and how badly it had gone with each of them. They were curious to know how it had gone with Martin. When they came from the hunt, said Martin to them:

"Ha! ha! Come on and eat till you are filled! Then I will show you the bird that made you both sick. A pair of clever men you are to let such a miserable creature overcome you!—Ha! Ha!"

Now they all sat down to the table, and ate till noon. Martin had cooked so well, that the Smith and Tailor kept praising him. After the meal, Martin said:

"Let us go and find Mannikin Long Beard. I have put him in a good prison, and paid him back. You shall see whether he is your fellow or not."

But what had happened?

When they reached the tree-stump,—ha! ha! ha! Mannikin Long Beard was not there! He had pulled so hard that he had pulled his beard out by the roots. He was gone, and had left his long beard in the stump. Ha! ha! ha!

HA! ha! ha! Ha! ha! ha! laughed the merry Wizard with the golden bushy head, pointed eyes, and apple-red cheeks, as he finished his Wonder Stories from the Amber Land.

146

THE VANISHMENT!

BOOM! BOOM! BOOM! BEAT! BEAT! BEAT!
Boom! Boom! Boom!

And Jakamas of the golden bushy head, pointed eyes, and apple-red cheeks, from Lithuania of the fragrant amber, thus ended his Wonder Stories.

And the Four Ancient Wizards were silent!

See! The Great Nischergurgje with a rolling and a roaring struck his Magic Drum. The tent door-flap lifted of itself. The glaring sun looked in, hot air filled the tent, and clouds of mosquitoes and gnats darted in buzzing and biting.

The Lapp children laughed and sang. They ran shouting out into the green valley, to gather strawberries and flowers, and hear the cuckoos calling. Birds twittered in the boughs, and streams and rivers sang sweet music.

And the Lapp tent grew higher and higher, and Nischergurgje, that tree-tall, tree-straight one, rose up. His white reindeer robe fell from his shoulders, and he was clad all in bright silk embroidered with variegated colors. He lifted his golden drum-hammer and again struck his Magic Drum with a rolling and a roaring.

Boom! Boom! Boom! Boom-i-ty boom!

A clap like thunder! The living speaking Kantele began to play of itself. The Four Ancient Wizards each struck his own Magic Drum—thump!—and vanished in smoke.

147

Then Nischergurgje, chanting Magic Spells—beat! beat! beat! and striking his Magic Drum, departed. Through the green flowering valley he strode, over mossy tundra, over shaking, quaking bogs, across flowing rivers, gurgling streams, and still lakes. The hot hot sun burned night and day in the Arctic summer sky. And all green things grew, grew, grew, night and day.

Onward and ever onward marched Nischergurgje toward the mountains, beating! beating! beating! chanting! chanting! chanting! whistling! whistling! whistling! Higher yet he climbed to the mountain-peaks from which he came.

And there Nischergurgje, the Great Lapland Wizard, sat him down to wait till the autumn with its gold-brown birch leaves was passed-to wait till the hot summer was gone and the Long Night was returning to Lapland—to wait till the Polar storms threw a veil of smooth white snow over valley and tundra—to wait till the Northern Lights were shooting once more across the dark night sky—flickering, wavering, darting here, darting there, amber-colored, red, orange, yellow, green, blue, violet flashings!

Boom! Boom! Boom! Beat! Beat! Beat!

In Lapland when the Arctic Storm Wind roars down from the mountains and through the valleys and blows over the plains do you hear the Call of the Magic Drum?

Calling! Calling! Calling!

Boom! Boom! Boom! Boom! Boom! Boom!

INTERESTING THINGS

THE TINY HISTORY OF THE BALTIC SEA

Pirate Days

RING! RING! RING! TOLL! TOLL! TOLL! The alarm bells were ringing, over twelve hundred years ago; along the east coast of Britain they were ringing and tolling. The Baltic Pirates were coming.

The British children, and their fathers and mothers saw the long, gilded, dragon-prowed pirate-ships come flashing through the billows of the North Sea. Painted ships they were, high-pooped, each with a spreading square sail and oars that dipped and rose and dipped again. Shields hung along the bulwarks; swords, spears and axes bristled on the decks. The stiff gale blew the Pirates' flowing red or blond beards and tossing locks. Helmets shone, birnies glittered, and icy blue eyes gleamed. Gigantic, huge-limbed, bold, were the heathen Pirates from the Baltic Sea, shouting praises to their gods, Thor and Odin. Vikings we call those Pirates.

And when the British children and women saw them coming, they ran about hunting for places in which to hide. The British men got out their pikes to defend their homes and children.

And after the Pirates' raid was over and the British homes lay sacked and smoking in ashes, back across the North Sea, through the winding channels into the Baltic, sailed the Vikings, their ships laden with rich booty. To the lands of Denmark or Sweden, or to the coast of the Saxons and Angles, the Vikings sailed their ships and anchored in home-harbors, till ready for another raid. Many were the raids made during hundreds of years.

And the Vikings themselves had to watch for Pirates. For there were Rovers on the Baltic, in those days, who preyed on the Vikings. From time to time brave red-haired Finns fell upon the coast towns and villages of Sweden, and made many a successful raid.

In those far-away days, the lands encircling the Baltic, were swarming with countless heathen Tribes of different races. The lands could scarcely feed them all. And the desire for bold adventures, for booty, for battle, for new homes in strange lands—with broad acres, plenty to eat, and a chance to rule—was strong upon the restless, fierce folk of the Baltic.

The Moving Hordes

IN those tumultuous days, the Baltic was not merely a protecting haven for Pirates. From its swarming beehive of peoples, went forth Tribes and Tribes and Tribes again migrating southward till at last they overwhelmed the mighty Roman Empire.

And from the Baltic shores sailed Saxons, Angles, and Danes who founded England in the British Isles. And in later days, English descendants of those same Baltic conquerors, crossed the Atlantic and helped colonize North America.

To go back to those far-off times of the Vikings, the peoples who did not leave their homes on the Baltic shores, but stayed to build cities, towns, and fleets of ships, became strong nations. Hundreds of years passed, and, in the Middle Ages, the Baltic was a centre of world commerce.

The Great Amber Sea

AND the Baltic is the Amber Sea.

Long, long ago, at the dawn of history, before the Birth of Christ, the Ancient Greeks used to buy a mysterious, beautiful substance, hard, light to lift, transparent like honey-drops, or of a milky yellow or clear, rich, red-brown color.

When they rubbed the substance, forth came a curious fragrance. When they burned it, up shot bright flames with a pleasant odor. And when they rubbed it again, lo! it was charged with an energy like that of the lodenstone, attracting objects to it. They were making the first electrical experiments, those Ancient Greeks, but they did not know it.

Nor did they know where the marvellous stuff came from. The Phoenician sailors had brought it from the coast of Gaul. The Gauls said that they had got it from the Tribes who dwelt near a northern water. They did not suspect, those Ancient Greeks, wise as they were, that the stuff—amber—was a petrified gum from the pine forests buried for unknown ages under the waves of the Baltic and in the amber-beds of its coast.

And if you admire amber, "the balsam of the forest, the gold of the sun, the shining of the water, the tin gling freshness of the breeze, when the world was young," you may read more about it in the Tiny Dictionary.

The Baltic Nations Today

TODAY, great Christian nations descended from heathen Vikings and the Baltic Tribes of old times rule the Baltic Sea. A number of them have no sea-outlet for their ships to pass to other lands, except through the Baltic. That Sea is a great centre of world-trade.

The Baltic measures about 160,000 square miles. Its waters are nearly tideless, almost saltless, and in places quite shallow, and are warmed by the Gulf Stream. In the northeast lie thousands of islands and islets.

The Baltic stretches one long finger northward between Sweden and Finland, and becomes the Gulf of Bothnia. It points another finger westward towards Russia, between Finland and Estonia, and becomes the Gulf of Finland. It presses a finger into Latvia's coast, and is the Gulf of Riga.

As for the nations and races of the Baltic shores, get out your map and count them. They are many—German, Polish, Danish, Swedish, also Russian, and all those interesting peoples living on the eastern coast.

And it is those interesting East Baltic folk, Finnish, Estonian, Latvian, and Lithuanian, who have told the stories in this book. So if you want to know about the Lapps who belong to the Republic of Finland, and about the Northern Lights, Lapp Reindeer Kings, Finland's thousand lakes and isles, Estonia's wonders, Latvia and Lithuania of the Amber Coast, and of many strange Baltic Things, read the Tiny Dictionary. Read it through! It is like a story—a true one!

GOOD BOOKS ABOUT EAST BALTIC LANDS

If you are eight or ten years old, read:

Birch and the Star, by Thorne-Thomsen. Row, Peterson.
Stories of children in Finland and Norway. Some of them are by Topelius.
    Zacharias Topelius, the Finnish author, loved children, and wrote
    fairy tales for Finland's children. Very beautiful tales they are!

Canute Whistlewinks and Other Stories, by Topelius. Longmans.
Translated by Foss, edited by Olcott, eighteen of Topelius' most beautiful
    wonder tales. Some of the titles are "Canute Whistlewinks," the
    boy who had for supper, pearls and seafoam, hot bar-iron, and fairy
    dewdrops; "Sampo Lappelill," the Lapp boy who rode the reindeer
    with Golden Horns; "The Princess Lindengold," and the Lapland
    Wizard; "Star Eye" and Lapp magic.

154

Friends in Strange Garments, by Upjohn. Houghton.
In this charming little book, there is a story about the Great Amber
     Road to the Amber Coast. The other stories are about children of
     different lands.

Top-of-the-World-Stories, translated by Poulsson. Lothrop.
Lovely tales, from Topelius and other Northern writers. Some of the
     stories are "Knute Spelevink"; "Princess Lindagull"; "Sampo
     Lappelill"; "Legend of Mercy"; and "The Forest Witch."

If you are ten or fourteen years old, read:

Finland and the Tundra, by Walter. Peeps at Many Lands Series.
     Macmillan.
A travel book with colored pictures, about the Finns and their Arctic
     neighbors, the Samoyads.

Good Stories for Great Birthdays, by Olcott. Houghton.
Contains stories about the Lithuanian-Polish patriots, Kosciuszko and
     Count Pulaski.

Kalevala, the Land of Heroes, translated by Kirby, Everyman's Library, 2
     volumes. Dutton.
The great Finnish poem about the Wizard Vainamoinen, and other
     Finnish wonder-heroes. If you like Hiawatha, you may want to
     hear this read aloud. When you are older, you will enjoy reading it
     yourself.

Sampo, by Baldwin. Scribner.
How the Magic Sampo ground out its treasures. How the Finland Wizards
     wrought their Spells. From the Kalevala, told in prose for children.

Troubadour Tales, by Stein. Page.
This contains one story, "The Lost Rune," telling how Elias Lonnrot
    went about among the Finnish peasants, gathering folk-songs. He
    published them in his book, the Kalevala.

If you are sixteen or over, read:
(These books were not written for young folk, but they are interesting.)

Beyond the Baltic, by Scott. Butterworth. (London)
If you like amber, you will find a delightful chapter here, telling many strange
    things about "Amber! The gem that not merely shines and glows, but
    diffuses fragrance round." Contains a map of the Amber Coast.

Finland and its People, by Medill. McBride.
An up-to-date, short travel-account of modern Finland, its life and aims.
    Illustrated with maps and photographs. If you ever tour Finland, be
    sure to take this with you!

Land of the Midnight Sun, by Du Chaillu. Harper.
If you borrow these two fat volume from the Public Library, you will
    revel in the Northern Adventures of the romantic traveller, Paul
    Du Chaillu, and in his many woodcut illustrations.

New Masters of the Baltic, by Ruhl. Dutton.
About those new Baltic Republics, Finland, Estonia, Latvia, and Lithuania.
    A book of travel, illustrated with photographs.

With Fire and Sword, by Sienkiewicz.
Translated from the Polish, tells about the struggles of the Poles, Lithuanians,
    and Cossacks. A powerful historical novel. Reading it, one imagines he
    can hear the march of Cossack hordes over the steppes. One seems to live
    in those tumultuous and terrible times, so vivid are the descriptions.

156

THE TINY DICTIONARY OF
STRANGE EAST BALTIC THINGS

AMBER: A storm on the Baltic! Tangled seaweed tossed upon the shore! And in the seaweed, lumps of yellow amber! That is what happens, and has happened for thousands of years. Amber is the fossil gum from extinct trees long buried under Baltic waters. And deep in the shore itself, lie rich deposits of the honey-colored substance. Most of the amber comes from the Baltic Sea. From amber, are made beads, mouth-pieces for pipes, cigar-holders, trays, cups, penholders, knife-handles, and incense. The fishing and digging for amber is an important Baltic industry. If you visit Lithuania and walk along the seashore, you may pick up handfuls of raw amber-lumps!

AMBER ROAD: The great amber-beds of the Baltic lie east of Danzig, and extend along the coast of Lithuania to Latvia. This region is called the Amber Coast. On page 217 you may read how the ancient Phoenicians procured amber. In later days, the Greeks and Romans traded for amber through merchants who travelled to and fro along a trade-route running from Latvia southward. This trade-route was the Amber Road.

AURORA BOREALIS: The Latin name for the Northern Dawn, beautiful Northern Lights flaming and flashing through the Polar Night. They are thought to be caused by magnetism from the earth's surface.

BALTIC PROVINCES: Before the World War, the three countries, Courland, Livland, and Estland, were called the Baltic Provinces of Russia, the country that ruled them then. After the War, these Provinces became Independent Republics—Courland and Livland formed the Republic of Latvia, while Estland became the Republic of Estonia.

BALTIC SEA: The Amber Sea.

ESTONIA: Also spelled Esthonia. Estonia is the officially recognized name of this Republic. In days unknown, before the Birth of Christ, strange heathen Tribes migrated, probably from the Ural Mountains, to the Baltic shore. These Tribes were different in language and race from the folks of Western Europe. About the ninth century, a part of these Tribes wandered to Hungary; they are called Magyars. A large division of these strange people had settled earlier on the Estonian peninsula, before the seventh century. They are the Estonians. Then a part of these Estonian settlers moved northward and made homes in the land of a Thousand Lakes; they are called Finns. These people, the Finns, the Estonians, and Hungarians, brought a wonderful gift to the other peoples of Europe—the love of rich colors and exquisite design, and of deep sad music. in the thirteenth century, the Sword-Brothers, the Order of German Knights, overran Estonia, subjugated her, introduced Christianity, and became the noble ruling class of that country. Later Sweden conquered Estonia, and ruled for about a hundred years, till Russia took Estonia and annexed her to the Russian Empire. She then became one of the three Baltic Provinces. After the World War the Estonian farmers and workers declared their Independence. February 24, 1918. Estonia is now a Democratic Republic.

ESTONIAN REPUBLIC: This new Republic is developing a trade along modern lines. Reval, its capital city, lies at the gateway of East Baltic commerce. The Estonian farmers raise rye, oats, barley, and potatoes. Much of the country's wealth is in live stock, and the principal exports are flax, paper, and timber. Estonia has ancient cities and towns, an educational system, and a system of railroads. The University of Dorpat is renowned for its learning. Estonians are music-lovers, and have produced some of the most beautiful poesy of Europe. Estonia is larger than Belgium or Denmark.

FINLAND: "The Land of a Thousand Lakes!" On a large map of Finland you can count many thousands of beautiful lakes and many many thousands of islands, whole archipelagos of them along the coast, and isles and islets dotting the lakes large and small on which float in the summer the wild, golden water-lilies. Swami is what the Finns call their land, which means Marsh Land. And Suomi is also a land of waterfalls, cataracts, and streams; dense forests of birch, pine, fir, alder, and aspen. The coastline is jagged, for the Baltic has carved out many a bay and sound. In winter the days are short and cold, long and bitter, but there is moonshine at night and the Northern Lights flash in the sky. There are winter picnics, sledging, skating, and skiing. "A meadow of wild flowers," is Finland in the spring and summer, and the "land of strawberries," and also of luscious raspberries, huckleberries, cloudberries, and clotted cream. A happy land for children!

FINN FOLK: The Finns, like the Estonians and Hungarians, are different in language and race from the peoples of Western Europe. The Finns are a vigorous people, with blue eyes, reddish hair, and high cheek-bones. They are a patient people, faithful, honest, thrifty, and most hospitable. They are freedom-loving and patriotic. Like the Estonians, they delight in music; and like the Estonians they came under the rule of Sweden and Russia. During hundreds of years past, Swedes have settled in Finland, and form an important part of the population. The descendants of Swedish settlers are called Finlanders. Finlanders, though Swedish in blood, belong to Finland heart and soul. Both Finnish and Swedish are spoken. Finland is larger than the British Isles.

FINNISH REPUBLIC: After the World War the people of Finland, both Finns and Finlanders, declared their Independence from Russian oppression and together with Finnish Lapland, set up a Republic,

159

December 6, 1917. Today, Finland is one of the most progressive States in Europe. Her ancient city of Abo, is called "the cradle of Finnish culture," while her capital, Helsingfors, is the seat of a progressive government, and of a University of high standing. Finland's agricultural and manufacturing industries contribute richly to the world's supply of dairy products, fish, paper, wood-pulp, and timber. The factories and sawmills are run by Finland's "white coal," which means the rushing waters of her streams, yielding electricity for her engines and steam for her boilers. And Finland has her own art and literature. Her native rugs, hand-woven of old in rich colors and delicate designs, are the envy of art collectors. As for the Kalevala, the Finnish national poem, it expresses the deep, melancholy, mystic soul of the Finnish people.

KALEVALA: A long, wonderfully musical Finnish poem about Wizards and Magic. It is composed of ancient heathen songs called runos, never written down, but sung from memory, by one generation to another. In latter times, some Christian ideas have been added to the runos. These native songs were being forgotten and lost till a few years ago, when Elias Lonnrot, a patriotic author of Finland, went about among the Finnish peasants listening to their songs. In this way he saved a large number of the songs, and published many of them in the Kalevala. Kalevala means the Land of Heroes. Longfellow so liked the Kalevala, that he modelled his Hiawatha on it.

KANTULE: Waterfalls, streams, and rivers murmur, tinkle, and sing the summer through in the Land of a Thousand lakes. The Finns speak a soft musical language. Is it a wonder then, that the Finns of old delighted to make sweet sad music on the kantele, and sing their mystic runos? The kastele, still used in Finland, is a small flat stringed instrument something like a little harp, held on the lap while the player draws his hand across it, and accompanies the wild, weird songs of the runo-singers. Two runo-singers sit facing each other, clasp hands, and sway rhythmically as they chant. First one sings a line, then the other repeats its meaning in different words. You will find this repetition in the Kalevala and in Hiawatha; also in the little verses in this book, which have the Kalevala rhythm.

LAPLAND: See "the Dancing Woman" on your map of Europe. She is Finland. Her tossing arms, head, and the upper part of her body, are Finnish Lapland. Lapland, as a whole, is a vast area, a section of which belongs to Sweden, and another section to Norway; but the largest section of all forms a part of the Republic of Finland. And what a desolate barren place Lapland would seem, were it not for the white beauty of the snow, and for the moonshine of the Long Nights, and the flaming of the Aurora splendor. The short summer, very hot, when the sun never sets, or sets for a brief while only, is made lovely with flowers and birds, and hideous with shaking bogs and clouds of thirsty mosquitoes. "Immense are the stretches of forest there, mighty are the rivers, and the mountains are higher than in the rest of Finland." Trees do not grow in the far North and the wild tundra stretches over great barren tracts. Lapland is a mighty and somber land. Its products are reindeer meat, skins, and cheese.

LAPPS: The short, nimble, dark-skinned people of Lapland, with triangular faces, flat noses, and high cheekbones, call themselves the Sameh or Samelats. We call them Lapps, which means wanderer or nomad. The Lapps, in race, are like some Arctic Tribes of Asia. Their language is something like Finnish. In the dim past, the Lapps probably wandered from Asia into Northern Europe. Over the vast area of Lapland, are scattered about 30,000 Lapps. Some live by fishing in the Arctic Sea and Lapland's rivers; they are called Coast Lapps, and dwell in villages or in lonely shack. Others who live by reindeer herding, must follow the reindeer herds from grazing ground to grazing ground, and move their tents and goods along with them. These tent-dwelling nomads are called Mountain

Lapps, for some of the best pasturage lies in the mountain valleys. Many Finnish Lapps are farmers, dwelling in little farm-houses. The Lapp loves bright colors, and his reindeer skin clothes are gaily embroidered. He hangs little tinkling bells on the shaft of his sledge, and drives his reindeer furiously over the snowy tundra, while the bells jingle merrily. He likes weird stories, and is easily frightened and becomes angry over very little. Though a Christian, he still believes in strange heathen things, like Magic Spells. But he is kindly, and hospitable.

LATVIA: Also called Lettland. Here is another new Baltic Republic, neighbor of Estonia. In early days some folk of the same race as the Estonians, dwelt in this land, but they have nearly died out. The present leading people are descendants of Lettish settlers, and are not of the same race as that of the Finns, Estonians, and Hungarians. The Letts and the Lithuanians belong to a mysterious European race living from ancient times on the Baltic. The Letts, or, as we call them now, the Latvians, have a most interesting language, while the history of their country is much like that of Estonia. Before the World War, the two countries, Courland and Livland, were Baltic Provinces of Russia. After the World War, the poeple of Courland and Livland united, declared their Independence, November 18, 1918, and set up the Republic of Latvia. The united people are now called Latvians.

LATVIAN REPUBLIC: Because of the charming, romantic scenery in some parts of Latvia, the country is called, "the Baltic Riviera." Another section of the country is known as "the Livonian Switzerland." Picturesque scenery, castle ruins, lakes, and lovely landscapes delight the traveller. In other sections, are forests and peat bogs, while farms dot the country, for Latvia is an agricultural land. Her capital city, Riga, is a railway centre for traffic from Estonia, Lithuania, Russia, Poland, and Germany. Through Riga's sea-port passes a world commerce. Latvia exports qauntities of flax, butter, poultry, eggs, honey, preserved fruits, fruit juices, paper and lumber. Latvia is spending large sums to educate her people, and there are a national museum, a state art museum, a national opera, and modern progress along many lines.

LETTS AND LETTLAND: See, LATVIA.

LITHUANIA: A living language, much like the ancient Sanscrit, that dead language of India, spoken today by a European people! What a marvel! Such is the language of Lithuania. Since long before the Seventh century, the Lithuanians have lived on the Baltic Coast. The Roman author, Tacitus, in the second century wrote of their "amber land." The Lithuanians are a fair-haired, fair-skinned race, a quiet agricultural people. But this quiet people have a remarkable history. Like the Estonians, they suffered under the scourge of the Sword Brothers. But unlike their Baltic neighbors, they were once mighty warriors. Indeed, Lithuania, about 1400, was the leading Ruling Power of eastern Europe. Since then she has suffered oppression under both Poland and Russia. After the World War, she declared her Independence, February 16, 1918, and set up a Republic.

LITHUANIA REPUBLIC: Lithuania is still hard pressed by her neighbor Poland. But she is brave and determined, and is peaceably defending herself from aggression. Meanwhile she is developing her trade and industries, organizing a school system, encouraging her national theatre, art, and literature. Lithuania's chief exports are live stock, eggs, poultry, meat, dairy products, and amber.

LIVONIA: Also called Livland. It is now a part of Latvia.

MIDNIGHT SUN: The farther North one goes in winter, the longer the night and the shorter the day, till beyond the Arctic Circle, there is a winter period during which the sun never rises. The farther North one goes in summer, the longer the day and the shorter the night, till beyond the Arctic Circle, there is a summer period during which the sun never sets. Now below the Arctic Circle, in the lower latitude, the sun just before midnight, in midsummer, sets for a few minutes, then rises again in brilliant splendor. This midsummer rising and setting of the sun is called the Midnight Sun. Read the lovely story of two children who saw the Midnight Sun; "When the Bright Sun Rises," in Canute Whistlewinks, by Finland's great author, Topelius.

MIDSUMMER NIGHT: Midsummer Day, is June 24. On Midsummer Eve, all fairies and elves are supposed to be playing about and witches to be flying round. In ancient days, the pagan folk used to worship the sun on Midsummer Night. They built bonfires and danced, leaped and howled round them, and jumped through the flames. Many peasants in Europe still build these bonfires, and dance and sing round them, and even leap through the flames. They say that they do this in honor of Saint John the Baptist. But they are really keeping up the old pagan rite of adoring the sun-god Baal. Baal-fires these bonfires are called. In Finland thousands of bonfires are kindled on Midsummer Night. In Latvia, besides building fires, a pretty flower festival is kept, which used to be held in honor of the Lettish cupid. In Finland there is a legend explaining these fires: The Sunset and the Sunrise begged the Lord of the sky to let them wed. So once a year, on Midsummer Night, at midnight, they clasp each other in glowing arms.

MOSQUITOES: In all Northern countries where there are bogs and swamps, mosquitoes are a terrible pest. In Finland and Lapland, in hot weather, mosquitoes swarm in clouds.

NAIL OF THE NORTH: A Lappish name for the Pole Star.

NORTHERN LIGHTS: See, AURORA BOREALIS.

PEIPIS LAKE: A large lake between Estonia and Russia.

REINDEER: A wonderful sight is a great gray herd of reindeer galloping over the hills, their bells tingling, their many branched antlers tossing. In winter they dig deep in the snow with their forelegs to get at their favorite food, reindeer moss. When a reindeer is harnessed to a sledge and is speeding over the snowy tundra, his spreading

164

hoofs keep him from sinking into the snow. In winter tha wandering Mountain Lapp moves his goods by sledge. But in summer, when the tundra is wet and boggy, he loads his pack reindeer and leads them along in a string. The reindeer herds supply the Lapps with meat, milk, cheese, and skins to use instead of cloth.

REINDEER KINGS: A rich Lapp counts his wealth by the number of reindeer he owns. Poor Lapps have only a few deer. Rich Lapps have large herds of sometimes a thousand or two thousand deer. Very rich Lapps are called Lapp Kings.

SAINT JOHN'S NIGHT: June 24 is supposed to be the birthday of Saint John the Baptist. An old pagan festival is still celebrated on this day.

SEITE: Lappish idol made of a huge stone found in some strange shape.

SKIS: A pair of long slender runners usually of birchwood, to bind to the feet, so that one may easily run over the snow or leap down hillsides.

SLEDGE: The Lapp sledge is called a pulka. It is boat-shaped, and when drawn rapidly over the snow by the swift reindeer, it rocks violently from side to side. But if it had runners, it could not pass so easily over all kinds of ground, bumpy, hilly, and flat.

STALLO: A man-eating Giant in Lapp stories, who is so stupid that any bright Lapp can easily outwit him.

SUOMI: See, FINLAND.

TUNDRA: The wide treeless plain near the Arctic Sea. In winter it is frozen. In summer it is wet and boggy. Reindeer moss grows on the tundra.

ULDAS: A kind of fairy folk in Lapp stories, man-size, and usually invisible.

VIKING: This word means sea-rover, sea-robber, pirate. It does not mean a King of any kind.

WIZARDS: The Red Indian has his Medicine Man, the Eskimo has Shamans, the African Negro has Witch Doctors, and the Lapp has his Wizards—and all of these magicians are supposed to control bad and good spirits, and to be able to throw spells on folk. They are usually great rogues and practice trick magic. The Lapp Wizards used to be very powerful men keeping the poor people in great fear of their spells. They used to beat magic drums pretending to call upon spirits for help and advice. Christian teaching has done away with much of this superstition, and the magic drum is no longer used.

THE END

CPSIA information can be obtained
at www.ICGtesting.com
Printed in the USA
BVOW06*2157040717
488497BV00008B/24/P